Satan's Coming to Town
By
Joshua Griffith

Contact Joshua Griffith on Facebook

Follow him on Twitter

Or on BookBub

Author Joshua Griffith's Official Webpage

Table of Contents

Chapter One

Mischief Is In The Air

Dennis grumbled to himself as he took his spot as the official Santa letters sorter. Christmas was a busy time of the year for the post office, with all the letters and packages tripling the normal rate. He sneered as he reached into the mail basket and snatched a handful of letters, still irritated that he was *volunteered* for the task this year.

Like all letters, each one goes through the postal sorting machinery, the Santa letters are sorted and then hand vetted by a postal worker in a separate area, away from the regular mail. Dennis's job was to ensure that the Santa letters had the official address set down by the post office:

SANTA CLAUS

123 ELF ROAD

NORTH POLE 88888

Operation Santa, as it was aptly named, started almost a hundred years ago as letters to the jolly ol' St Nick came pouring in from children across the country. The program evolved over the years, letting postal workers, random citizens, and charity groups open the letters and make a child's wish come true. Now, people all around the world could go to www.USPSOperationSanta.com to be a secret Santa. Dennis didn't care for the holiday itself and anything related to it. He was happy that he didn't get the tedious task of putting all these letters online.

Dennis looked around, not seeing the 'Discard bin', and huffed, "How do they expect me to do this without proper equipment?"

Letters that didn't have the proper address or only had the North Pole or Santa written on the envelope got discarded. If Dennis had his way, he would take a metal barrel out back, dump all the Santa letters in it, and set it on fire. Dennis knew that there was a chance that non-Santa letters could be in these mail bins so the fire was on the back burner, so to speak.

He examined the letters in his hand and chuckled, seeing the misspelled name of Santa, in red crayon.

"Might have a better chance at getting Satan to grant your wish, kiddo, because it's garbage now."

A heavy hand landed on his shoulder, startling Dennis. He knew exactly who it was, which caused his mood to sour further, just from the man's cologne. "What do you want, David? Can't you see that I'm busy?"

David laughed merrily as he came around to face Dennis, "I can see that. You've barely clocked in and you're already in the weeds."

"It should've been *you* doing this job, not *me*!" Dennis growled.

"It's not my problem," David shrugged his shoulders slightly with the wisp of a mocking smile, "That's what seniority can do for you. A shield against the shit shifts. One day, you'll be able to do the same."

"Why are you here? Is it your intent to mock me?"

David calmly replied, "Far from it. I'm here to inform you that there's a special bin coming for all the undeliverable Santa letters."

"All I see are these overflowing bins here," Dennis motioned to the five mail baskets. This was just the beginning and he knew that more were coming. "What's so special about the bin?"

"I haven't heard much." David stated as he absentmindedly perused the letter. "Just that the higher-ups want to make sure no kid gets left out. Frankly, I don't know how they can feasibly accomplish it."

Dennis snorted, "That's the problem with them! Always looking for more ways to make our jobs tougher. I would love to see any one of them come in here and do it. It's not possible! The little brats can't be bothered to use the proper address, let alone spell it right. I got several letters for *Satan*. Maybe *he* can do it."

Both workers let out belly laughs that could rival the fictitious holiday icon. As the laughter died down, a small female approached the men, carrying a big red plastic bucket.

The woman was small and seemed to be swallowed by her thick winter jacket. The hood covered her head and was lined with faux fur, obscuring her face. She placed the bucket on the sorting counter. It suctioned itself to the countertop like it was specifically made for the surface.

The woman said with a melodious voice, "Special delivery and Merry Christmas!"

"What the hell is this!" Dennis cried out indignantly, "Do the big wigs believe that this bucket can handle *all* the crap letters?"

"I'm just the courier, not the one with the answers." The lithe female replied as she skipped away. The little holiday bells glued to her boots grated on Dennis's nerves.

David picked up the special container and examined it, "You're right. I don't see this holding all the letters. You're going to have a hell of a time with it. I wonder what these strange markings on the sides mean?" He glanced at Dennis and then chuckled, "Glad it's you and not me."

"Gee, thanks," Dennis flatly replied, "Either help me or get out, but I already know the choice you've made, so leave."

"Fine," David set the red bucket down on the countertop. It moved of its own accord and suctioned itself to the surface as the two postal workers glared at one another. "Enjoy my gift to you. Merry Christmas."

"Piss off! Next year, you'll be doing this. Mark my words, David!"

Before he exited the door, David turned and flashed his co-worker a knowing grin, "Good luck with that," he gave a quick nod towards the bins, "Better get to it. Those letters won't sort themselves."

Dennis grumbled under his breath as he tossed several letters in the special container. The music was getting on his nerves. Nothing but Christmas songs were blaring over the speakers. He could have sworn that he heard Mariah Carey's *All I want for Christmas is you* at least three times since he clocked in less than an hour ago.

It's bad enough listening to this crap and it only adds to the stress of this damn holiday!

Dennis tossed more letters in the special container and each time he did this, the little etchings on it would glow and pulsate. The postal worker rolled his eyes.

More gimmicky Christmas shit, Dennis mentally muttered, *it's bad enough with all the garland decor and twinkling lights in this place. Did they believe a glowing box would be fun to see?*

Dennis was tossing letters around like he was on autopilot, barely registering a voice speaking to him. He jumped when he felt a small hand touch him on his bicep.

"Crap, lady!" He snapped, "Announce yourself next time!"

"I did. You weren't listening."

Dennis realized that it was the same woman that delivered the special container. He narrowed his eyes at her and asked angrily, "What do you want? Back to bring more work for me? Can't you see that I'm swamped?"

Deep from inside her heavy hood, the female locked eyes with Dennis, staring him down without uttering a word. His anger lessened and a feeling of calm washed over him. Dennis gulped as he said softly, "I'm sorry, miss. I didn't mean to be so crass."

The lady giggled, which had Dennis captivated. He wanted to see what her face looked like without the massive hood encasing it. There was something about her that he couldn't figure out, something not quite right.

"You're not a fan of this time of the year, are you?" The woman asked, her voice was both soft and playful.

Dennis sheepishly rubbed the back of his neck, "Nope. I find it stressful and filled with unneeded pressure to buy things for people. I'm Dennis, by the way."

She reached out to shake his hand. Dennis took her hand into his and noticed how soft and delicate it felt in his massive calloused grip. He feared that his squeeze could break her fragile hand like a potato chip but, to his surprise, her grip was stronger than he could have imagined.

"I'm Cheesahdew. Nice to meet you."

Dennis cocked his head to the side with a puzzled expression, "Cheesahdew? I've never heard such a unique name as that. Does it have a special meaning?"

She let go of his hand and slowly pulled back the heavy hood. Dennis let out a soft gasp, taken aback by her pure beauty. Cheesahdew had long flowing black hair as fine as silk that pooled around her lightly bronze face. Her face appeared delicate; petite with no blemishes. Her eyes were a light brown that seemed to twinkle, which had Dennis wondering if it was the Christmas lights glinting causing this mesmerizing sight. Her nose was so small that it reminded him of a newborn and her lips were thin and glossy.

"It means *Rabbit* in Cherokee."

"So, you're a Cherokee as well?" Dennis asked.

"You could say that," Cheesahdew answered, the corners of her lips rising in a slight smile. Dennis stood there before her, speechless. He felt like she was special in some way and it had him puzzled as to why she was standing here before him. She broke eye contact and looked down at the letters beside him on the countertop.

"Does that letter say what I think it says?" Cheesahdew asked as she pointed.

Dennis turned and glanced slightly, knowing which one she was referring to, as he smirked, "Yes. Satan is on a lot of the envelopes. They'll end up discarded unless it has the official address for the North Pole."

"Seems like such a waste of a good wish," Cheesahdew said as she stepped up to the countertop.

Her fingers gently caressing the different envelopes. Dennis could not help thinking about her hands touching him. The way she moved was both sensual and with purpose. She could not have been no more than twenty. He was twice her senior, but that did not prevent his mind from wandering or his eyes from ogling her form when she wasn't looking.

The postal worker snorted, "That falls on both the children and their families for not ensuring that the letters have the correct address on them. It's out of my hands."

"So, you say, but I think that you could do more if you truly desired," Cheesahdew replied as she circled around him, her hand brushing his back like a lover, causing Dennis to shiver. "Would it be such a terrible thing to put the proper address on the envelopes?"

The postal worker stuttered under her scrutinizing gaze, "I-I wish that I could. The thing is, well, I don't have the time for it. Sorting these letters is my top priority. I don't enjoy it so I'm not going to go out of my way to amend them either."

Cheesahdew walked over to the red bucket, the little bells on her shoes jingling and somehow, sounded like they were mimicking the song *Jingle Bells* to Dennis. She leaned down and whispered inaudibly to the special container. The etchings on it glowed brightly for a moment and then went back to normal. Confused, Dennis was about to say something but she playfully put a finger against his lips and said, "In that case, I'll leave you to your work. I'd *hate* to be a distraction, but I'd happily be one *if* you did as I asked."

She smiled as she felt him kiss her finger. Cheesahdew took it off his lips and slowly licked where Dennis's lips had touched it. He let out a low groan, imagining many inappropriate thoughts.

"So young, and yet, set in your stubborn ways." Cheesahdew stated as she turned to saunter out of the room.

"Young?" Dennis let out a belly laugh, "You're kidding, right? I'm damn near sixty. I'm old enough to be your father, little lady."

Cheesahdew turned to look at him over her shoulder, her black silk hair flowed like it was alive, and smiled coyly, "Looks can be deceiving, Dennis. Maybe, if you're a good little boy, I might swing by later and you can show me what it's like to be my *Daddy*."

She swayed her hips as she lifted her hood up over her head, causing the postal worker to lustfully growl, which made Cheesahdew smile. Dennis's mouth gaped open as he watched the young lady leave, his eyes fixated on her tight ass. His mouth was parched at the thought that she wanted him. Dennis turned around and went back to work, hoping to get through all the letters so he could have a chance to get together with her.

Cheesahdew stepped outside in the cold, harsh winter weather. She walked around the corner of the building and down into a short alleyway.

She leaned her body against the brick wall, looking all around at her surroundings and smiled, "Humans are so much fun to play with. This should be an interesting Christmas this year. Let the fun begin."

Her body contorted as her features distorted. The winter clothing that Cheesahdew wore loosened greatly and dropped in a heap on the pavement. She pushed her way out of the discarded clothing and hopped forward. The young lady had transformed into the body of a rabbit. It stood on all fours and was two and a half feet tall with gray fur with white patches.

Cheesahdew stood up to her full height and cheerfully said as her little nose wiggled, "One post office down. Plenty more to go." The trickster rabbit left the alley with inhuman speed and then disappeared completely.

Chapter Two

Delivery!

Deep down in the darkest depths of Hell, the cries of the many anguish souls reverberated everywhere. Sulphur permeated the stagnant, muggy air. The realm was lit brightly, using massive torches the size of a Winnebago that constantly moaned in eternal anguish, which were fueled by the souls of the damned, as part of their punishment.

The darker the soul, the worse the punishment became. Despite the lighting, there were more shadowy areas in Hell; places that even the bravest of demons wouldn't tread. Not because of some of the unspeakable monstrosities that lurked in these dark spots…but from glitter.

It was said that EnergyBear, a Cherokee god of creation and mischief, had sent every dimension and realm where demons resided, including Hell, packages with glitter inside them. It didn't matter if someone opened it or not, the packages exploded, releasing the contents. Demons and other entities didn't trust that anything *good* would come from this god. The glitter seemed to have a mind of its own, which had many entities, especially demons, wary of it.

The sparkling STD of the crafting world was now just as big of a deterrent of demons as was salt. The denizens that reside in Hell heard rumors that if you get this *divine glitter* on your body, it either burns like acid or it simply made entities look like festive idiots.

Lucifer didn't mind this at all. In fact, the fallen angel uses it as punishment for any of the unruly demons. He watched over Hell like a prison warden as his devils mete out the appropriate punishments for each damned soul. The fallen angel didn't want anything to do with humanity, let alone their eternal souls, but he had a job to do. Once in a while, Lucifer would take a damn soul to work over before handing it off to one of his skilled torturers.

Much like his Father was to Heaven, Lucifer was, in a sense, a god in Hell which gave him more freedom than any of the other creatures residing there. Nothing escaped his angelic sight, nor his senses.

The ruler of Hell observed Sorath as he scurried around the *Landscape of Sorrow* completely naked and looking haggard. Lucifer chuckled as the soap on a rope around the neck of his fallen angelic brother snapped off once more, fear etched on his face as his punishment was about to continue.

"Hmm," Lucifer mused, "I'm curious as to what will have its way with Sorath this time?"

Just behind the fallen angel appeared a massive creature. Its body was bound within a flesh-and-blood form with thick rocks covering it in various places, like armor. It didn't have a humanoid head, but it had six tiny eyes and a gaping, circular maw full of razor-sharp teeth.

Sorath's eyes widened as a pair of massive hands gripped him by his shoulders, its thick, obsidian claws dug painfully into his flesh as it bent him over a jagged, magma-covered cluster of stalagmites. The molten rocks scorched Sorath's flesh as he was impaled on them while the bulking creature sexually assaulted the angel roughly. The creature hunched over Sorath's back and, using its maw, viciously tore into the crook of his neck.

"A behemoth," Lucifer chuckled to himself. "Well, brother, looks like you're in for a long, painful evening. Maybe next time you'll think twice about violating our sister Purah."

Lucifer's amusement was short-lived. He furrowed his brow, feeling a disturbance in the warding of Hell. The ruler of Hell didn't like unwanted guests, but whatever it was that came through didn't have a pulse.

The fallen angel commanded, "Bexuc, come here!"

A tall, muscular built upper-level demon appeared from thin air, kneeling on the floor with his clawed hands touching the hilts of his swords. Bexuc looked up at his master and asked coldly, "Whom am I to dispatch, sire?"

"Something has breached Hell without my consent," Lucifer answered, his voice was a combination of calm, cold, and melodious. He flicked his fingers and a small crystal ball hovered in the air. "Go here and retrieve whatever it is. Bring it to me so that I can figure out who sent it so that you can dispatch the responsible party."

Bexuc stood up, his gaze fixed on the crystal ball. Lucifer noticed a flicker of fear briefly crossing the upper-level demon's visage.

"Something wrong?"

"No, my liege. Nothing that I can't handle," Bexuc answered curtly and then he disappeared.

Lucifer stared at the spot where Bexuc was and said, "Fear. What exactly is it that would cause him - oh!" It dawned on him as he chuckled, "It's located in the *Shadowy Void*."

Several minor demons stood mere inches from the shadowy fissure in the brimstone wall. They nervously glanced at each other as sweat glistened on their thick, black leathery skin.

One pointed at the *Shadowy Void* and nervously asked, "What was that flash? There's nothing in Hell that's bright enough to pierce that kind of darkness, is there?"

"You saw it too?" Another one asked, "Do you want to go in and see?"

"No! That's the *Shadowy Void*!" The smallest of the impish demons cried out in panic, "Don't you know what lives inside there?"

"A glitter beast," Bexuc answered coldly, causing the minor demons to yelp with surprise. He stood before the massive fissure and unsheathed his swords. The upper-level demon gulped loudly, "Our master wants the item that entered here. I *must* go in and you three are joining me."

Each demon lowered their heads, nodding as they said in unison, "Yes, Bexuc."

They had no choice. If an upper-level demon commands a weaker demon, they *must* obey or die. The minor demons moved in front of Bexuc, forming a protective line. If the glitter beast decided to attack, the minor demons would be the first to go.

The little imps each looked back at Bexuc, worry and fear coated their goat-slitted eyes as he ordered, "Move!"

The minor demons warily marched into the *Shadowy Void.* The sounds of their footfall soften the further they advance. The temperature fell drastically, causing all the demons to shiver. Bexuc wasn't sure what to expect in here. The *Shadowy Void* had always been here; the perfect place to escape the non-stop wailing. Ever since the strange glitter arrived, few had dared to enter.

Those that did enter were covered in the shiny stuff or were eaten by the glitter beast. Bexuc, like many of the other demons, pondered which was the worse fate of the two. The glitter was sentient and none could predict what just one small piece would do. Why the fallen angel allowed it to stay, the upper-level demon couldn't say, nor was it his place to question it.

Darkness shrouded them, causing a sense of claustrophobia. Sensing the fear in the minor demons, Bexuc snapped, "Keep moving forward! You don't want to get lost in here."

Something pulsated up ahead, Bexuc knew that it had to be the item his master wanted. A sense of foreboding and being watched entered their minds as the demons stopped near the glowing object. The sound of sand pouring surrounded them, which meant one thing: the glitter beast.

Bexuc lifted his bony chin up and stated, "Dweller of the *Shadowy Void*. My master requires that I take that to him at once."

The sound of sand blowing in a small room echoed with its laughing, "Does he now? What does he offer us in return?"

"I was not aware that an exchange was to be made for *his* property." Bexuc sneered at the beast indignantly.

"It fell here, so technically it's *my* property. I require a finder's fee."

The upper-level demon bristled as his body stiffened. Through gritted teeth, Bexuc asked as politely as possible, "Fine. What do you require?"

The glitter beast coalesced, surrounding the demons in a sparkling circle, despite no discernable light source to make it occur. It morphed into a visage of a bear; its maw was big enough to swallow an entire demon with little effort.

"Just how badly does Lucifer want it?" The glitter beast asked as it eyed the demons intently, enjoying them squirming under its scrutiny.

"Lucifer wants it because it's not normal for refuge to enter Hell. I imagine that he will grant whatever you desire." Bexuc answered as the glitter moved closer to the group. He debated on teleporting out of here, but the master wouldn't be pleased if he knowingly disobeyed his command.

"It's obvious what I want. I *hunger* for demonic playmates. Which of you wants to play with me?" The glitter beast chuckled.

Without warning, Bexuc kicked one of the minor demons forward and announced, "Dexile is up for some mandatory fun!"

The minor demon glared at Bexuc as he rubbed his ass. He turned his attention to the shiny creature and saw that its sparkling visage was a foot away from him.

The beast inhaled deeply and then asked, "What do you taste like, little one? Are you nice and tender so my teeth can easily render?"

Dexile shrugged his well-defined muscular shoulders and said, "I'm not sure. I suspect that I am for one such as yourself, but," he motioned with his head, grinning, "everyone knows that if you want flavor, the meat needs to be aged. Bexuc has been around for centuries. I say eat him too, if you plan on eating me first."

Bexuc snarled but as he reached for the minor demon, the glitter beast snatched him. It lifted the upper-level demon up in the air, dangling Bexuc over its opened maw as it stated, "Let's find out, shall we?"

Bexuc dropped into the creature's mouth. His screaming was heard each time the glitter beast opened its mouth to chew. The minor demons recoiled as they watched Bexuc's flesh being ripped apart by the individual pieces of glitter.

The glitter beast clamped its maw shut, smiling down at the minor demons. Movement on what would be considered its cheeks let them know that Bexuc was still alive.

The glitter beast grinned, "You were correct. This one is quite the delicious morsel."

"So," Dexile tentatively asked, "What's to be our fate?"

The glitter beast spat Bexuc onto the floor, his flesh and muscles were shredded, exposing the various bones. The upper-level demon was profusely bleeding ichor all over and had glitter lining his numerous wounds. Bexuc glared at the minor demon as he tried to get up, but his legs and arms couldn't support his weight.

A decent size cloth sack was tossed on the upper-level demon's back by the glitter beast as it said with a chuckle, "Take this to your master. Either take your friend with you or let him slink out of here on his own. Payment accepted. You may go in peace and love."

As the glitter beast slithered away, Bexuc reached a gnarled arm towards the minor demons and croaked out, "Help me...you fools...Take me...from here..."

Dexile grabbed the upper-level demon by his fleshless hand and yanked his arm off. Bexuc howled in agony as more black ichor spilled from the wound as the little demon crunched the appendage together and beat Bexuc with it until he was unconscious.

Dexile turned to the other demons and ordered as he twirled the deformed arm like a baseball bat, "Grab the bag and meet me at the master's chamber. I need to help our dear friend out of here."

The other minor demons meekly nodded as one of them walked over and hesitantly grabbed the sack. The heavy bag stuck to the mangled flesh and muscles like it was held there by a sticky glue. After several tugs, the sack came free with a sickening pop. The two demons looked at Dexile for a moment, wary of leaving him behind.

"Go. I must take Bexuc's power for myself," he eyed the two minor demons, daring them to challenge his claim, "unless either of you wish to lay claim to it."

"Not at this time," one hissed, but then he lowered his voice, fearing that the glitter beast would return, "And definitely not in *this* place."

"Then wait for me outside Lucifer's chamber," Dexile barked. The two minor demons flinched but obeyed, turning to leave the *Shadowy Void,* dragging the ichor-stained bag with them.

Dexile turned his attention back to the unconscious upper-level demon. He rolled over Bexuc's sticky body and then he straddled his torso. With his claws, the minor demon carved small sigils across Bexuc's chest while muttering an incantation in his demonic tongue. The upper-level demon grunted painfully as he opened his one good eye and muttered, "What...are you... doing…?"

"I'm consuming you and all your power. By right, I can claim it since you can't fight me off," the minor demon smugly replied and then went back to his spell work. Dexile punched his fist into Bexuc's chest and grabbed a hold of his heart and squeezed, digging his claws into the tough muscle.

Bexuc gasped as he attempted to buck Dexile off of him but to no avail. The upper-level demon could feel both his magic and life force leeching away into the other demon.

"Stop!" Bexuc half consciously pleaded to his attacker, "Don't do..."

The upper-level demon's head lulled to the side as he died. Dexile maniacally smiled as he pulled the heart out and slowly consumed it. With each bite, the minor demon could feel his impish form growing in size and strength. Dexile's body thrummed from the influx of strong magic, his eyes rolling back in his head.

After a few minutes, Dexile opened his eyes fully and stood up. He noticed that he was standing taller and his muscles were bigger and had more definition.

The demon cackled as he walked away, mocking Bexuc, "Enjoy the *Shadowy Void,* Bexuc. Your new tomb for all eternity."

Chapter Three

The Letters

The two minor demons anxiously awaited for Dexile to join them. They had no choice but to obey him. It was obvious that he had bested Bexuc with his devious cunning, using the glitter beast as his weapon of choice. Demons consume power in order to grow stronger, whether it's from people or other demons, and rise up in the hierarchy.

"How strong do you think Dexile is now, Tybus?"

"He won't be the same as he was before we entered the *Shadowy Void,* Rux," Tybus answered honestly as he looked down at the heavy sack, stroking his chin, "I wanted to challenge him but his body was already consuming the upper-level demon's power and surpassing mine easily. I can only imagine what he's like now."

"Together," Rux conspired with his counterpart, "we can overtake him and grow. I'm sick of being on the bottom of everyone's boots!"

"That attitude will *always* keep you in your station," Tybus admonished, not completely dismissing Rux's assassination plot. The idea of taking both Rux and Dexile's power was enticing so he added, "Still, you have validity in your argument. We should talk later from prying ears. A plan is needed."

Rux bent down and sniffed the heavy sack. He pawed at it and shook it, trying to figure out what was inside it, "What do you think is in here? What's so important that we had to risk our lives for it?"

"It's not our place to question Lucifer's orders," Dexile answered as he appeared out of thin air. The minor demons looked up at their friend and were both shocked at his transformation.

Dexile grew at least three feet taller and seemed to be glowing with a black aura. "He wants it, then consider it a privilege that you get to hand this over to him with me. He will reward us all accordingly, which is why I wanted you both with me. I want all of us to grow."

Tybus chuckled as he pointed at him, "One of us already has done that. Maybe we should go in without you so that we can catch up."

In an instant, Dexile had both minor demons by their throats. He hoisted both of them off the ground.

His black eyes glaring coldly into their fearful eyes, "*Don't* take me for a fool! Your thoughts betray you both. I know you both want what I now possess! I'll give you both a chance for it after we deliver the master his prize. We were forced to do this so we *all* deserve his gifts. Do we have an understanding?"

Both minor demons nodded hastily as they both grunted, gasping for air. Dexile released them, letting them drop to ground in a heap.

He reached over and plucked the heavy sack up and said, "Good. Come along."

Rux helped Tybus up and they fearfully bowed to their friend. Dexile walked confidently towards the throne room with Rux and Tybus following behind him. The door to the throne room opened as the demons approached it, unnerving each of them. The demons had never been inside nor been this close to the fallen angel. Only a select class of demons and the devils got that honor.

"Bring me what I asked for. I'll not ask again," Lucifer bellowed, his impatience blatant.

All three demons snapped out of their fearful state and rushed inside. The throne room was a chamber that Lucifer could change at will, depending on whatever he needed at the time. Today, it resembled an oval-shaped office. Books and movies decorated the walls, along with pictures and posters from various movies and TV shows that depicted him in them. There was an old record player that had *Sympathy for the Devil* by the Rolling Stones softly playing.

Dexile put the sack on the marble floor and backed up, kneeling with the other two demons. Lucifer was standing with his back to them, looking at a projector screen. It had images of humans on it of various ages.

"Of all of these people," the fallen angel said aloud, "which one of them plays me the best?"

"Sire?" Dexile questioned, feeling confused.

"It's a simple question," Lucifer said as he half turned to face them. He waved his arm at the screen, "Which one of these actors plays me the best? Tell me that you know what I'm talking about?"

In unison, the demons shook their heads, each one shaking in fear.

Was this a test, Dexile wondered?

"Pity. To think that I created Comcast just so we could have free entertainment. Sometimes I wonder why I even bother to keep my minions happy. I mean the customer service alone was a stroke of torturous genius." Lucifer flatly stated with a sigh as he walked over and kneeled down to examine the sack. He glanced up at Dexile and said, "I see Bexuc failed the task. Tell me, how did he fall?"

"The glitter beast demanded payment in exchange for the sack," Tybus answered, gulping audibly, "Bexuc offered us as payment, but–"

"But what," Lucifer asked and then he frustratedly ordered, "Stand up and face me! I don't like talking to scalps!"

"Dexile outwitted him, sire," Rux chimed in, hoping to deflect the fallen angel's ire." Made the glitter beast eat Bexuc."

"Did he now?" Lucifer said as he stood up. He slowly walked around the demons, never taking his gaze off Dexile. He stopped in front of the bigger demon, towering over him with his eye glowing white, "And how did you manage to pull that off? Bexuc *was* a favorite of mine."

Dexile mentally glared at the other minor demons. He wanted to kill them both here and now, but Lucifer's presence made him fearful.

He gulped, feeling like this was the end, "I did what needed to be done to procure your prize from the glitter beast. I offered Bexuc to it, reasoning that it would prefer to eat an aged demon. It accepted the offer, chewed him up, and spat him out. By right, I claimed his power and his life, my master."

"You cunning little demon," Lucifer chuckled, "His own fault for ordering a devious one such as yourself to do his bidding. This is what you found for me?"

Dexile was surprised that the fallen angel didn't smite him. He quickly masked it and recovered by answering, "Yes, my master. That is the source of the disturbance."

Lucifer turned and grabbed the sack. He untied the string rope and pulled open the hole and was puzzled by the contents. The fallen angel lifted the sack and dumped out a massive amount of envelopes on the floor.

"What in the name of *Me* is all this?" Lucifer said aloud. He snatched up one of the letters and added as he scratched his head, "Do I have a fan club that I don't know about?"

The minor demons and Dexile approached cautiously, looking at the envelopes with curiosity. Lucifer opened one and pulled out a letter, his lips moving slightly as he read it to himself. He turned the letter over, examining it to see if there were any more words on it. Over and over, the fallen angel opened each one and discovered that they had one theme in common.

"These are Christmas letters, addressed to me?" The fallen angel said, feeling confused.

"Not my place to ask," Dexile spoke up, holding one of the envelopes in his clawed hand, "but has this ever happened before?"

Lucifer glanced at the mid-level demon for a moment and said as looked back at the crayon scribbled words, "Do I really need to answer that, Dexile? Nothing from Earth comes down here, except souls, yet somehow this bag of children's letters made it here."

"Perhaps someone is mocking you, sire?" Rux offered.

"He has a point, master," Tybus added, "Christmas letters. What better form of mockery could there be by sending you letters celebrating the birth of Jesus?"

Lucifer chuckled, "I can see the irony, if it were true. He wasn't born on the day that the humans celebrate His birth on. The point of the holiday was to get more of the pagans to convert to Christianity, since they celebrate Yuletide a few days earlier. It's amusing to watch them bickering about it, especially when none of them know *when* my old friend was born. I should know because I was around when my Father sired Him. Scandalous, it was. A virgin getting pregnant! Oh, it was fun listening to *those* conversations in that little quaint domicile."

"So, what are you going to do with this rubbish?" Rux asked as he kicked the letter pile.

Lucifer's eyes glowed brightly white as he used his hand and magically forced the minor demon away. With the snap of his finger, all of Rux's skin ripped off his small body.

The other demons cringed as Lucifer coldly remarked, "The letters belong to *me*. You disrespected me the moment your insignificant foot touched them. Now, clean up your mess or I'll do something far worse than that."

"Y-Yes, s-sire", Rux painfully bit out.

"Tybus!" The fallen angel ordered, causing the minor demon to flinch as he stood at attention, "Go get Paroxysm for me, *now*!"

"Right away, master!" Tybus responded, running as fast as his little legs would allow. He glanced over at Rux and cringed as the other minor demon meticulously picked up the pieces of his flesh, groaning in pain with every movement.

The mid-level demon looked at the pile of letters and asked, "What are you going to do with these letters, sire?"

"Gather them up and put them back in the sack. We're going to take a little trip with them," Lucifer said, reading another letter carefully once again. He could feel that magic was used to get this delivery down into his domain, but Lucifer couldn't say exactly who did it. It felt odd and strange that so many children had written *him* Christmas letters, but it amused him.

Dexile hoisted the mail sack over his shoulder and asked, "Where are we going with these?"

As Tybus strolled in the throne room with Paroxysm just behind him, Lucifer eyed them both and said, "All of you, bundle up for the cold weather. We're heading to the North Pole."

Chapter Four

Meeting with the Jolly Fat Man

"Paroxysm, my dear! I'm so glad that you could spare a moment from your soul torturing to join us." Lucifer jovially called out.

"It's not often that I get a break from my *happy place,* even lesser is an audience with you, my liege," the she-devil replied with a slight nod, her voice was smooth as silk, but her personal demeanor was far from it, "What is thy bidding, Lucifer?"

Lucifer glanced at her, pointing at the skyless void above them, and said, "I need to know what the world is like up there. I rarely have the opportunity to see it personally, so your knowledge on this little field trip will be invaluable. As my favored she-devil, you get the worst of the worst souls to flay and torture, which grants you more knowledge than most."

"I'm honored to be of assistance," Paroxysm replied with a slight smile. She glanced over at Rux, who was carrying his skin out the door as she added, "Forgive me, sire, but what knowledge do you seek?"

"You need to come with us as I gather intel from the one known as *Santa*. Do you see the sack that Dexile is holding?" When the she-devil nodded, Lucifer continued on, "Those are children's letters, addressed to me, wanting Christmas gifts. I'll need you to guide me as to the meaning of each kind of gift because I don't know the proper protocols involved with this holiday. I know humans give each other gifts, but being down here has stunted my knowledge of this tradition."

"I see. Just know that it would be best to ask Santa for his list. It may shed more light on things that I may not have the answers to, sire," Paroxysm said as she walked over to Dexile. As she pawed at the mailbag, the mid-level demon glanced at the fallen angel for guidance.

Lucifer chuckled, "Let her take one out. Paroxysm needs to know what we're going to do. She won't defile them like Rux did earlier, will you, Paroxysm?"

The she-devil reached in and grabbed a random letter. She sauntered over to the fallen angel, causing the mid-level demon to groan as her hips swayed slowly back and forth. She handed it to Lucifer and said, "It's yours to read, not mine since it's addressed to you, sire. I'd say that these are like wishes from children, hoping for them to come true, which is why they write to Santa in the first place."

"Can't the parents fulfill these wishes? Why write to a supernatural stranger for things?" Lucifer asked as he pulled out the letter.

"Most offspring have parents that simply don't have the means to do it. They lack funding or just don't want to do it because of the same reason. People tend to rely on the kindness of strangers to do it, hence the letters, but the offspring don't know it." The she-devil explained.

"I see, and yet, it makes no sense to me. Which is why I need you for this. But first," the fallen angel swirled his hand, creating a portal, "we need to talk with Santa so I know what I must do, since I *must* answer."

"Wouldn't it be easier to hand them to Santa?" Tybus asked as he bundled up in the only winter apparel that could be found in Hell. Skin clothing, layered and stitched together, stuffed with entrails and muscles.

Lucifer nodded in agreement, "The thought did cross my mind, but like I said, these letters are addressed to me. So, it's up to me to fulfill the wishes of the little urchins."

Dexile set the mailbag down and teleported away after seeing the blizzard conditions through the portal. Lucifer asked the she-devil, noting that she didn't bother leaving like the other demons, "Do you plan on getting dressed for this or go as is?"

Paroxysm coyly responded, "Unlike them, I can let Hell keep me warm. That's why I've never needed any clothes. Plus, it helps with my interrogation sessions. The men love it and will spill their deepest, darkest secrets to me as I gut them, just believing that they *might* have a chance to touch me."

The fallen angel nodded curtly as Dexile reappeared, "Very well. Grab the bag, Tybus and don't drop it or you'll suffer worse than Rux."

The minor demon gulped as he scampered over and grabbed the bag off the floor. Dexile let out a soft sigh, grateful that he didn't have to carry it.

That's what the lowly minions are for, he thought, knowing that he was like Tybus not that long ago.

"Come along," Lucifer ordered as he stepped through the interdimensional portal.

Paroxysm motioned for the other demons to go next. She glanced at Rux as the demons went through the portal and said, "Clean every drop of your blood off the master's floor with your tongue. Make sure that you don't miss any or he *will* do far worse to you. Got it, imp?"

"Yes, Paroxysm," Rux replied as he groaned loudly.

The demon got on the floor and lapped up the blood as more dripped beneath him. The she-devil laughed as she walked through the portal.

The harshness of the arctic wind bit into them like a ravenous hellhound that hasn't eaten a person in a month. As they trudged through the calf-high snow, Lucifer kept glancing at the mailbag. Tybus was struggling under its weight as he held it on top of his head, trying to keep the contents inside from getting ruined by the snow.

The fallen angel stopped and barked out, "Take the bag, Dexile! Tybus can't handle it in the snow at his size."

"Yes, sire," Dexile replied with a slight groan as he rushed over and snatched the bag away from the minor demon. Tybus mouthed, "Thank you!" but the mid-level demon glared as he slung the bag over his shoulder.

"How much further?" Paroxysm asked as she effortlessly glided through the thick snow. The fiery heat emanating from her body caused the snow to melt, creating a small trench that the minor demon followed. Dexile grumbled, wanting to hand the mailbag back to Tybus now that he wasn't neck deep in snow, but he also didn't want to go against Lucifer's order.

"Not far. We should be at the edge of his pocket dimension," the fallen angel replied as several arrows landed before him.

He looked in the direction that they came from and saw a small group of ice elves; their bows notched with more arrows.

"That's far enough, outsiders! One more step and it will be your last!" A blue elf in a red uniform and green boots threatened.

Lucifer eyed them with boredom, "Then go fetch Santa for me."

"I'm no errand boy," the ice elf exclaimed as he aimed his weapon at the fallen angel.

"I don't care who you send," Lucifer replied, his eyes glowed white as he spread his ethereal tendril wings, "He and I have a matter that needs to be discussed. If you don't lower your weapons, I'll smite *all* of you where you stand."

Whispers and pointing ensued, but the leader of the ice elves only glared at the intruders. He was about to let his arrow fly when he felt a beefy hand on his shoulder.

"Stand down, Cuget," Santa said with a slight smile. He looked at the interlopers and asked, "What brings the ruler of Hell and a few of its denizens to my doorstep?"

All the ice elves, including Cuget, backed away a few steps as Santa stepped towards the fallen angel.

Lucifer pointed at Dexile and said, "I received a curious bundle of letters, addressed to me, asking for Christmas gifts. Did you send them to me as a form of jest?"

Santa jovially chuckled, "No, I didn't. I *receive* letters, I don't send them. If these letters upset you–"

"What do I do with them?" Lucifer snapped, "I don't know what to do with them, let alone know how your little holiday works so show me your infamous list and I'll be on my way!"

"There's no need to get worked up over them," Santa held his hands up, trying to placate the fallen angel, "Why do you need my list? It doesn't say anything about the gifts that the children want."

Lucifer glanced at the bag for a long moment and said, "Most don't have addresses on them. I don't want any of the little urchins to get left out because of a small technicality."

Santa stood next to him and put his hand on the fallen angel's shoulder, causing both the demons and the she-devil to protectively hiss, "Most don't. I have the magical ability to find them nonetheless."

"Dexile!" Lucifer commanded, "Bring me the bag." As the mid-level demon handed it over, the fallen angel added, "Since you have that talent, add your tracking magic to them."

"This isn't your holiday, it's mine, Lucifer. I can handle these letters easily enough," Santa said, trying to reason with the ruler of Hell.

Lucifer yanked his shoulder away from the jolly man and proclaimed, "Fuck that, fat man! These letters are addressed to *me* so *I'm* doing it. Are there any rules that I need to know about?"

"Such language can easily get you on my naughty list!" the jolly man tsked as he shook his head in disapproval.

Lucifer raised an eyebrow and, with a deadpan expression, replied, "You realize who you're talking to? I'm the reason you have your list, you judgmental prick! I'm the original naughty boy. I should know because you've *never* brought me any gifts."

Santa sighed, "All this fuss over a few misspelling mistakes."

The fallen angel slipped his hand into the bag and held it to the jolly man's face, "Little Billy doesn't know that! As you can plainly see, he asked for *Satan*, not *you*!"

Santa dismissively waved his hand, "There's nothing to it. Give them what they ask for. It's as simple as that, Lucifer. Whether you get the exact item that they asked for can vary, depending on what it is. You have to do your run on Christmas Eve. Let me tell you, that's not an easy feat, even for a small order that you have there. Hmmm, I believe that I recognize the magic that's been used on these letters."

"Who's magic is it?" the fallen angel asked.

He wanted to meet the one responsible for this mess and throttle them. Santa eyed Lucifer for a moment and then it dawned on the fallen angel what the jolly man said, "What? But that's tomorrow? One fucking night to deliver *all* of these? What kind of nonsense is that? This ranks up there with me losing my golden fiddle to a fucking hillbilly."

Santa raised his eyebrows and asked with a jolly chuckle, "A golden fiddle? Where did you acquire it?"

Lucifer shrugged his shoulders, "Long ago. Before recorded time of Man. A fella by the name of Keith Richards."

"He's *that* old?" The jolly man replied with surprise.

"Yes. He was accompanied by a stunning blonde named Betty White, but their true identities are written in the first book by my Father as Adam and Eve."

Santa shook his head in disbelief. He looked at the fallen angel and composed himself, "As I was saying before we took a trip down memory lane, it's the only rule for the holiday. Like I said, if you're not up for it–"

Lucifer threw his hand up, cutting Santa off, "No! I said that I'm doing this and that's final. The little urchins asked, so I *must* treat it like any deals that's brought before me. Now, who sent these to me?"

Santa eyed Lucifer with a twinkle of joy, "It's the trickster known by the Cherokee people as Rabbit."

"Another trickster mocks me? A damn *bunny* is to blame?" The fallen angel scoffed, "I'll skin it alive and then I'll–"

"Gifts first," the jolly man said, pointing at the mailbag, "torture later. If you don't want to disappoint the children, then I suggest you go and prepare. It's going to be a long night."

"Fine. I'll send some of my minions out to fetch this Rabbit. It will wish that it hasn't trifled with me," Lucifer stated as he turned on his heels. With a wave of his hand, he created a new portal and furiously stormed through it with his minions in tow.

The fallen angel strolled over to his throne, fuming as he steepled his fingers under his chin. He looked at Dexile and ordered, "Gather who you need to and subdue the trickster. I'll be putting a bounty out on this Rabbit. The trickster will have very few safe harbors when word spreads about the price on its head! Take a few hellhounds with you to track it down, but don't kill it."

The mid-level demon approached the throne as Lucifer held out a piece of one of the envelopes, "For tracking, sire?"

"You may have taken Bexuc's power, but obviously not his intelligence. Take it before I choose another to go in your place and you can stay here and be my hellhound's personal chew toy!"

Dexile grabbed the piece of paper with a shaky hand and then teleported away. Lucifer sighed loudly as he read the letter to himself.

This Rabbit will not get away with this!

Paroxysm walked over with her head slightly bowed. The fallen angel glanced her way and said, "Since I'll be taking you with me, make sure you dress appropriately. The little urchins don't need to see all of your exposed flesh. I'll summon you shortly."

"Yes, sire," the she-devil nodded as she teleported away. Lucifer sat in total silence as screams of anguish echoed off in the distance; contemplating how he was going to pull this Christmas run off.

Chapter Five

New Addition

Lucifer stood before a shimmering bone-framed mirror meticulously adjusting his white suit. A smirk appeared on his angelic visage as the thought of wearing a red cape, a horn tail while holding a crimson pitchfork for the night. Maybe a hoop headband with horns and cloven hooves like a satyr?

Too much?

He chuckled while clipping his star-shaped cufflinks. Lucifer may be a fallen angel, but he was still an angel. Not the image humans portrayed him to be, which was a super villainous satyr.

Lucifer had only himself to blame for it. Long ago, the fallen angel appeared before a bunch of monks that had one too many goblets of wine, dressed up in that attire purely for his own amusement.

The ruler of Hell didn't expect these inebriated holy men would actually write down what they had witnessed. From that moment forward, *that* was how humanity viewed Lucifer. An absurd caricature from a prank.

At least it made me memorable, Lucifer thought to himself.

The fallen angel was clad in white leather, from his pants to the vest and tunic underneath it, that contoured to fit his body perfectly. His jacket was crafted from material that was stronger than steel and, at the same time, softer than silk. The black calf boots that were tucked under his pants had a pristine shine and could easily keep any ice and snow out and were stylish.

Lucifer turned around when he heard someone clearing her throat. He was about to speak, but paused before any words were uttered. Paroxysm stood before him, wearing a short jacket that resembled Santa's coat as a one-piece dress with a black belt fastened together by a gold buckle. The she-devil also has hunter green thigh high boots and a Christmas cap to cover her horns. Instead of the usual fluffy ball at the end of the cap, a strand of mistletoe dangled.

Lucifer finally said with a shrug, "At least you have clothes on."

"It's been some time since I've been on Earth," Paroxysm replied as she ran her hands up and down her body, "I figured that this would make for a clever Christmas disguise."

"I'm sure that it will do. Who knows, you might break a few hearts and steal some souls before this night is over."

Paroxysm's crimson eyes lit up with excitement, "Can I keep them if I do? Oh please, please, please, say yes!"

"I suppose, since it's a time for giving," Lucifer replied with a slight shrug of indifference, "Call it a bonus for assisting me."

"Yes!" The she-devil did a little happy dance. The fallen angel rolled his eyes with a hint of a smirk. The ruler of Hell psychically called out to his minions to come. Many different types of demons and other denizens of Hell appeared, all bowing down before their master.

Lucifer paced back and forth before his minions with his hands clasped behind his back as he announced, "As you may or may not be aware, I must go to Earth and deliver gifts to children tonight because some trickster thought it would be a challenge. I can't do it alone. There's some orders that I alone must handle because the magic required will need my *special* touch. Any that chooses to assist in delivering these items that the children of Earth have asked for shall receive…"

All of the creatures held their collective breaths, waiting for what their master had to offer. Lucifer paused before them. A benevolent smile grew across his angelic visage as he said, "Whatever your blackened heart desires. I don't care what it is. Think of it as my Christmas gift to you. Any questions?"

A tentative tentacle lifted up as the serpentine creature asked, "How we find? What we give?"

The fallen angel had the mail bag drop at his feet. He held a smaller bag in one hand over it and a few letters slipped into it as he said, "The envelopes are magically earmarked with the signature of each child that wrote it. The more gifts you deliver, the better the reward for you, but a word of caution: Any of you that fails me and doesn't deliver what the child asks for will earn my ire for all eternity. Am I clear?"

The legion of creatures nodded in union as the fallen angel added, "Good. Take only what you can handle. I'll know when they've been completed because I've added my own touch to them. Now, go forth and make it happen! Nothing is off limits, but make sure not to cause *too* much trouble up there. Above all else, *don't harm the children* but any that gets in your way is fair game!"

The fallen angel stepped away and allowed his minions to pilfer through the mailbag. One by one, the many denizens of Hell disappeared with letters in their clutches. Lucifer placed a small magical bag that held all the special letters in it to better protect them and pulled the first envelope out.

The fallen angel concentrated on it as he opened a portal to the first address and said, "Let's get started, shall we?"

They both walked through the portal and found themselves in a small, barely lit apartment. Lucifer glanced around at the little domicile, noting that it was sparsely decorated for the holiday.

There were pictures on the wall, nestled in a space between two doors. Lucifer walked over to the door that said *Billy's Space* and opened the door. He saw the young boy wrapped up in a blanket, lying on his racecar bed.

The she-devil looked him over and said, "This child is special, sire."

"In what way do you mean?"

"I'm referring to a special needs child. One that is *different* from most children. His mind is on a different level of reality. Humanity doesn't quite understand it. They refer to it as *autism*. What did little Billy ask for?"

"A brother. One that he could play with and would not hurt him like other kids," Lucifer replied as he cocked his head to the side, eyeing the child thoughtfully. He could see into the boy's mind and saw how chaotic it was. Regular talk wouldn't work so he communicated with Billy mentally.

The little boy's eyes fluttered open. When he saw the two strangers in his room, Billy screamed incoherently to no one in particular.

Lucifer held up the boy's letter and mentally said with a soothing voice, "*I got your Christmas wish that you sent me.*"

Billy eyed him for a minute before shouting and clapping his hands, "SANTA!"

At that moment, Billy's mother and father rushed into the bedroom. The boy pointed with wide eyes, "Santa!"

"Who are you two and what the hell are you doing in our home?" The father demanded as his wife rushed over to Billy, holding him protectively in her arms.

"It's Christmas and I'm here to deliver presents to all those that wrote to me," Lucifer replied, holding up Billy's letter before the man's eyes, "Billy wrote to me and now I'm here to make good on what he asked for. It's quite simple."

"Santa isn't real!" The father growled as he picked up a wooden baseball bat, "Who are you? I'll not ask again!"

"Oh, Santa is real but I'm not him. As you see from the slight misspelling, he asked for Satan. Not his fault, but here I am."

Lucifer spread out his tendril wings, lighting up the room and added, "You'll know me better as Lucifer."

The father got between his family and the two intruders and, with a shaky voice, said, "I-I'll not let you take him! I'll die-"

"Stop being so melodramatic," the fallen angel sternly commanded as he let his wings disappear behind his back, "I would never harm an innocent boy like Billy. I'm just here to grant his wish and then we will be on our way."

"What did he ask for," the father asked as he glanced at his child. Billy was overly excited, making it difficult for the mother to hold on to him.

"His letter made no sense, but I was able to read his thoughts and discovered that he wants a little brother," Lucifer stated as his eyes landed on the mother.

The look of shock and horror caused both the fallen angel and the she-devil to chuckle. Paroxysm made lewd pelvic thrusts to add to the parent's discomfort.

"You can't be serious?" The mother bit out, "I can't have a baby with you!"

"This is true," Lucifer smirked, "It wouldn't get here in time for Christmas, so sex is out of the equation. I can tell that you're broken up about it, so I'll give him one. Would you like a *special* brother, Billy?"

"Santa!" Billy replied loudly.

"Very well," Lucifer said as his eyes glowed white. At that moment, a little demon appeared in the room, startling the parents. The imp kneeled down and asked, "What is your command, sire?"

"You see that little boy there?" Lucifer pointed at Billy. When the little demon nodded, he added, "From this night forward, you are Billy's new little brother. You will protect and watch over him until the end of his time here on Earth. Any that try to harm him, deal with them as you see fit. Morph into a form that won't frighten him or his parents and swear an oath of allegiance."

"I swear that no harm shall befall him under my watch. If it does, Paroxysm may deal with my punishment or you may smite me yourself, sire," the demon said as it transformed into a young boy with brown hair and dimples. The little imp shifted his eye color to a dark brown, concealing his black eyes the best that it could.

Lucifer looked at Billy and motioned for the boy to come over. The mother held on to him tightly and said, "No, Billy. Don't go to him! He's evil!"

"SANTA!" The boy cried out, fighting to get away.

Paroxysm leaned down next to the mother and coldly said, "Hurry up! We have more wishes to grant so let him go or I'll break your arms."

The mother reluctantly let Billy go. He scrambled off the bed and ran up to the imp and hugged him. The demon looked up at Lucifer uncomfortably, hoping for help, but got none from his master.

"BROTHER!" Billy exclaimed as he vigorously jumped up and down. Lucifer squatted down, mentally speaking to the boy. As he emphatically nodded, the ruler of Hell stood up and put a hand on Billy and the demon and announced, "Billy has accepted his gift. Scar is now bonded to him and is now a part of your family."

"How do we explain this to others? To our other family members?" The mother asked.

Lucifer pulled out another letter and focused on it. He shrugged his shoulders as he opened up a portal and said as he and Paroxysm stepped through, "That's none of my concern. Make it up or simply call it a Christmas miracle. Scar can easily communicate with Billy. Something you two are lacking in so he can help you understand him better. Merry Christmas, you hairless monkeys!"

Chapter Six

Sibling Fun

They stepped out of the portal and into a dark alley. The air felt damp and musty as several rats scurried away to a nearby dumpster. Lucifer looked around, trying to find the sender of the next letter when several men walked towards them.

Each man wore a leather jacket with spikes on the shoulders, fingerless gloves, and denim jeans. Paroxysm locked her eyes with each man; they all were leering at her like predators. She whispered to the fallen angel, "If you don't mind, I'm going to sample the local cuisine here. Let me know if you need my assistance, sire."

Lucifer looked at the men stalking their way and he replied with little remorse, "Don't get too gory. I don't want you scarring the children for life tonight. Those fools, you can scar and do whatever you wish to them. This one is easy to do. They belong on your rack."

Lucifer walked down the alley as he heard the men grunting and promising to do terrible things to Paroxysm. He laughed to himself as he heard her egging them on by telling them about the mistletoe and that she was cold and needed to get warm quickly.

The fallen angel noticed a set of steps leading down to a red door at the base of the large building to his right. It had a small pine wreath with a golden ribbon tied at the bottom. Lucifer stepped down and turned the knob as the men screamed from somewhere further away, but the door didn't budge. The ruler of Hell scoffed as he forcefully turned the door knob; a pathetic lock wasn't going to prevent him from making his deal tonight.

Lucifer strolled down the dingy tile floor, hunting for his next appointment. A scantily dressed woman sat on the floor, her back against the wall with a needle in the bend of her arm. She looked up at the fallen angel; her eyes glazed over as she said, "Hey big boy. You wanna party tonight?"

"No, I'm busy," Lucifer replied as he stepped over the woman's sprawled legs.

"Ah, don't be like that," the junkie pouted, "It's Christmas Eve. I can make it a memorable night for you. What do you say?"

The fallen angel looked down at her and said, "I'm good, but my friend will be here shortly. She can give you what you truly desire."

The woman lunged forward, grabbing him by his leg, and demanded, "I don't want a woman, I want *you*! Take me. Right here, right now!"

Lucifer sighed. He reached down and snatched the junkie up by her small throat. The fallen angel hoisted her up in the air, causing the woman to gasp and choke as he got her inches from his angelic visage.

The junkie's eyes bulged as Lucifer coldly remarked, "No means no. If you don't relent, I'll smite your emaciated form!"

"Yeah..." the female croaked out as she rubbed her crotch against Lucifer's leg, "choke...me harder, Daddy..."

Paroxysm stood nearby, licking the blood from her clawed fingers and remarked with a giggle, "You're right, sire. This Christmas wish *will* easy to fulfill."

"Be a dear and take care of this filth for me before she gives me something that the strongest of holy water can't cleanse away," the fallen angel said.

"Are you sure, sire," the she-devil comically snorted, "To me, this looks like true love. One could call it a match made in *Heaven*!" Lucifer only glared at Paroxysm, so she said, "Fine. Toss the little trollop over here and I'll deal with her."

The fallen angel tossed the junkie at the she-devil's feet. Lucifer turned on his heels and marched away, searching for his next delivery. He heard the woman's muffled crying before silence descended on the hallway. Lucifer used his senses as he tracked down the next child.

He stopped next to a door that had seen better days. It was scuffed up, had paint chipping off it in spots, and numerous indentations. Lucifer placed his hand on the beat-up door and forced the locks to click open. He gently turned the door knob and let himself in.

The interior of the apartment was no better than the door. The carpet had tears and was stained black like a huge ink blot. Cracks covered the walls like a topographic map of some river system and there were areas on the sheetrock that needed repair. The foul odor of cigarette smoke, alcohol, and rotting fruit permeated the stagnant air, but it didn't bother the fallen angel.

How they live is their own choice.

Lucifer walked over to a doorway that had no door at all. Just an old blanket with cartoonish animals on it was tacked to the top of the wooden framing. He stepped in and saw a young girl, probably no more than seven, sleeping on a thin mattress on the floor, curled up with a tattered sheet. Lucifer glanced down at the child's letter and was surprised that she didn't ask for a new house.

As he made his way to the sleeping child, Lucifer stumbled over an array of toys and clothing. The fallen angel ended up falling down on the floor, causing dust to plume up and sting his angelic eyes. The young girl sat up with a start, eyeing the strange man in her room. As Lucifer sat up on his knees, he scowled at the refuse on the floor. The child backed herself into a corner, using her tattered sheet as a last line of defense.

She sniffled softly as the fallen angel stood up. He adjusted his attire and then looked directly at the child and admonished, "You really need to keep your room tidier than this. A person could get hurt in here."

"That's the point," the young girl replied, sounding distant, "I have to know when the bad people come in here for me."

Lucifer looked around the room and saw nothing suitable to sit down on so he magically made a cushy chair appear. The little girl's eyes bulged, seeing the stranger do this and she asked, "Who are you?"

The ruler of Hell pulled out the letter and announced, "I'm here because you wrote me a Christmas letter. This is your letter, isn't it, Rachel?"

Rachel let her sheet drop as she crawled cautiously towards Lucifer, "Yes, it is. Are you Santa? You don't look like Santa."

"Very astute of you to notice. I'm not him. I'm Lucifer and I'm here to grant your Christmas wish."

Rachel cocked her head to the side and asked, "Why do you want to grant my wish for Santa?"

"Because little urchin," Lucifer explained as he handed her the envelope, "You misspelled the jolly fat man's name, which meant that your letter got sent to me. I'm Satan, as you humans love to call me. The Devil himself."

"Oh," and that was all Rachel said.

Lucifer eyed the little girl and asked, "Oh? That's all you have to say?"

She shrugged her bony shoulders as she sadly replied, "I've had worse people in my life. Why not you too, right? I suppose that I deserve it."

"What makes you think this way, child?" Lucifer asked, his curiosity piqued, "Do you believe that I'm here to punish you?"

"Why not? My mom thinks that I should be. That's why she lets my brothers do whatever they want to me. And the men she brings home..."

Paroxysm stepped into the room, her nose crinkled in disgust, "This is quite possibly the most malodorous hovel that I've ever been in, which isn't saying much. Is this the wisher, sire?"

"Who is she?" Rachel asked, eyeing the she-devil warily.

"This is Paroxysm. She's assisting me tonight," Lucifer looked over his shoulder, his eyes glowing white, "Be a dear and probe her mind. There's a few people that deserve your *special* attention."

"As you wish, sire," Paroxysm replied as she made her way to the small cot, stumbling every so often. She sat down next to Rachel and patted her lap, "Hop up, little one. I need to see who's been hurting you."

The girl looked at Lucifer hesitantly, but he encouraged her, "It's all right. She won't hurt you. You will feel a slight pressure in your head, but I promise you that neither of us will cause you pain."

"You promise?" Rachel asked as she bit her bottom lip nervously.

The fallen angel leaned forward, getting eye level with Rachel and said, "I may be evil incarnate to you humans, but there's one thing that I deplore the most and that's people who hurt little children in ways that make you feel dirty. I give you my vow that none will hurt you again and we certainly won't, Rachel."

Rachel nodded slowly as she carefully climbed up on Paroxysm's lap. The little girl leaned against her as a stream of tears trickled down her dirty cheeks and said, "I don't know most of them or their names."

"That's all right." Lucifer reassured the child, "Paroxysm has a talent for seeing pain. She will know who the culprits are and shall deal with them accordingly."

The she-devil sneered in disgust as she searched the child's memories. Rachel looked up at Paroxysm when she heard her grumble and sadly said, "I'm sorry if I'm upsetting you."

"You have nothing to be sorry for, child," Paroxysm replied, but didn't look at the girl. Her eyes were glowing black.

She didn't want to frighten Rachel so she closed her eyes and added, "You're the victim. The ones that hurt you and the ones that allowed it to occur are the monsters. Monsters that I've marked for punishment."

"Like my mommy?" Rachel asked, fidgeting nervously.

"Her too. She used you for her own personal gains. She doesn't deserve an ounce of mercy." Paroxysm said coldly, but then she opened her eyes and cheerfully said, "Now, let's see what Uncle Lucifer has for you tonight. Time for your present, Rachel!"

The girl cupped her mouth, stifling a squeal, not wanting to wake up her family. Lucifer looked up from the letter, stroking his chin and said, "It says here that you want a way to torment your siblings. Why is that, Rachel?"

"They like to pick on me. I can't stop them and if I try, I get in trouble. I don't want to hurt them. I just want them to leave me alone." She shrugged her shoulders in defeat, "I have enough to deal with already."

"I see," Lucifer remarked. He reached into his jacket pocket and pulled out a gold chain. It had a small pendant that looked like a twisted version of a horse. It glowing softly as the fallen angel whispered an Enochian incantation on it. He dangled it before Rachel and said, "Have you ever heard the term *nightmare* before?"

"Yes, I have them every night," Rachel said, her eyes transfixed on the jewelry.

Paroxysm sadly nodded at the fallen angel and asked, "I've seen them too, sire. Can I keep her? I promise to flay anyone who even looks cross at her!"

"Hell is not a place for a child and you know this," Lucifer sternly admonished, but when he looked back at Rachel, his face softened, "This little trinket doesn't look like much, but it will do whatever you want it to do for you. When you put it on, you can't remove it because it's your protection. You can call upon a Nightmare and it will do your bidding, either in dreams or reality. Put it on and I'll gladly tell you how to use it."

Rachel reached out and grabbed the necklace as Paroxysm benevolently smiled down at her. She examined it in rapt awe, tracing her tiny fingers over the intricate carvings. The child slipped the chain on her head and let it rest against her chest. It felt warm against her skin, even through her nightshirt.

"Right," Lucifer said as he vigorously rubbed his hands together, "now that you have it on, it has bonded to you. Meaning that you're the only one that can use it. You activate it by saying the Nightmare's name."

"What's its name?" Rachel asked, a look of excitement glowed on her small face.

"His name is..." Lucifer paused for a moment and then said, "Nevermind his real name. It's too long and complicated for you to speak so you may refer to him by the name Mr. Carrots! Try it. You need to introduce yourself to him after all."

"All right. Mr. Carrots!" The little girl squealed with anticipation.

The pendant flared brightly for a moment and then a wisp of black smoke billowed from it. The black smoke landed on the floor and slowly coalesced into the shape of a horse. The dark steed had fiery eyes and snorted puffs of smoke from its nostrils. Its hooves glowed crimson, like a fire was burning on the inside.

It snorted as Rachel rolled off the she-devil's lap and made her over to the beast. She reached out and gingerly touched the Nightmare. It felt hot to the little girl, but that didn't keep her from petting it.

Lucifer looked at the Nightmare and ordered, "Rachel is your new charge. Protect and watch over this little one and break her tormentors in whatever fashion you deem necessary. Are we clear on this, Mr. Carrots?"

The Nightmare nodded in acknowledgement and asked the child, "What is your request, Rachel?"

The little girl's eyes lit up in shock, "He-he can talk?"

"Of course he can!" The fallen angel replied cheerfully, "No point in having a one-way conversation. Just know that you can call Mr. Carrots forward by saying his name out loud or in your mind. He will keep you safe. So, what do you want him to do for you, Rachel?"

She looked at the Nightmare and said, "My brothers need to be taught not to pick on me. Can you help?"

Mr. Carrots' lips curled up in a malevolent smile, revealing several rows of sharp teeth, "Say no more, Rachel. By the time I'm done with them, they will be begging you for your forgiveness. Just know that only you can stop me, but I have no problem coming out on my own."

"Will I be able to ride him," Rachel asked.

"If need be, yes," Lucifer said as he stood up, "Don't be surprised if your tormentors have bite marks on them. The Nightmare needs to eat and meat is something that he loves. He can sustain himself on the dreams of others too, especially the bad kind."

"Will you eat my dreams," Rachel looked up at the dark steed, "I have a lot of bad dreams."

"I plan on it, Rachel. It's how we shall bond together. I will consume them to give you a proper respite," Mr. Carrots said as it bowed its long neck in a nod, "You will need therapy to help extinguish them fully, but for the time being, I'll buffer them from you. Now, if you'll excuse me. I have some siblings to torture."

The Nightmare shifted back into black smoke and shot out of the room. A few moments later, they could hear moaning and crying coming from the other rooms.

Lucifer looked at Paroxysm and said, "Delivery is done. On to the next child."

As the ruler of Hell stood up to leave, Rachel rushed over and hugged him on his thighs. Lucifer was taken aback as the girl kept on repeatedly gushing, "Thank you, Lucifer!"

He looked at the she-devil, imploring for her to intervene, but all she did was smile. The fallen angel tentatively reached down and patted Rachel on her back, "Okay, child. Lucifer needs to get back to work now. Off you go." When she didn't let go, he pointed, "Go to bed. Shoo!"

Rachel looked up at him and said softly as she wiped her eyes dry, "Sorry. You're the first person that's not tried to hurt me."

Lucifer jutted his angelic chin out and said, "The irony isn't lost to me. Now, off to bed with you."

Rachel rushed over and hugged Paroxysm and then shuffled over to her cot. As Lucifer opened up a portal, the little girl hesitantly asked, "Can-can I write to you again?"

"No, but you can get it to me through Mr. Carrots." Lucifer replied, feeling a strange sensation in his chest. He studied the child and asked, "Why would you want to in the first place? I'm evil."

Without hesitation, Rachel shot back as she laid her head down on her grimy pillow, "I know evil and neither of you are to me. Good night and Merry Christmas, my friends."

The child fell asleep, softly snoring as she clutched her new necklace. Lucifer glanced at Paroxysm and flatly said, "Humans are so strange."

"An act of kindness goes a long way with those that have never experienced it before, sire." The she-devil remarked as she eyed Rachel.

"Before you ask," the ruler of Hell turned to the portal he just created with the next letter in hand, "Yes, you have my permission to come back and see her"

The she-devil squealed with delight as Lucifer rolled his eyes while they both stepped through the portal.

Chapter Seven

Can We Keep It?

Upon stepping out of the portal, they were met with a bone chilling blizzard. Snow drifts were as high as their knees as the wind howled all around them. Lucifer looked up at the cloudy sky and bellowed, "You can turn off the bloody ice machine, *Dad*! Your mortals have plenty down here!"

"Did that make you feel better, sire," Paroxysm yelled out over the strong wind, "or will He *actually* listen to your request?"

The fallen angel sneered, "He doesn't listen to anyone, not even His own worshippers. My Father couldn't care less about humanity, why would He give two shits about me?"

The she-devil nodded as she shrugged her shoulders, looking around for their next stop. The house was difficult to see, the roof had so much snow on top that it looked like one huge snow wall. A small chimney with smoke wafting out of it was the only indicator that it was a house from their vantage point.

Lucifer used his hand and, with a magical burst of fire, melted a path towards the frozen domicile. Once they got close enough to the house, they could see through one of the condensation-covered windows that the occupants were awake in the living room.

Lucifer glanced at Paroxysm and said as they watched the family, "Let's go in and introduce ourselves, shall we?"

She nodded as he melted a path to the front door. Lucifer reached out to grab the door knob, but paused. The she-devil looked up at him and saw that the ruler of Hell was smirking as he knocked on the door several times.

He glanced down at her and said, "Might as well be polite and see if they will welcome us in from this terrible storm."

"Like we need permission," Paroxysm answered sarcastically.

A muffled male voice called out as he peered at them from a pane of glass on the door, "Yes? Can I help you two?"

Lucifer held up an envelope and said with a toothy smile, "Delivery for a Timmy Jones!"

The man narrowed his eyes suspiciously and replied, "Nice try, assbutt. The mail carriers don't run at this time of the night."

"Do let us in," the she-devil said with a pout, "It's so cold out here and we're freezing."

"I don't know who you two are but if you don't get off my property," the homeowner threatened as he showed the barrel of a shotgun to them, "I'll fill you both with buckshot!"

"Really?" Lucifer scoffed, "Is this sort of behavior what you want to expose your little urchins to on this holiday? Now, be a good little boy and open the door. We're on a tight schedule."

The door was yanked open, striking the wall hard. The man aimed the shotgun and was about to pull the trigger when he heard his wife call out, "Dave? Who's at the door?"

Dave glanced over his shoulder for a split second, which gave the fallen angel his opportunity. He reached out and grabbed the barrel of the shotgun and bent it upward like it was made of plastic. Dave's look of astonishment quickly transformed into fear as Lucifer's eyes glowed white, "That was quite rude of you, Dave."

Dave dropped the mangled weapon on the floor and backed away slowly as the two denizens of Hell walked inside. An older woman walked around the corner as Dave backed into her.

She looked at the two new *guests* and asked, "Dave? Who are these two? Friends of yours?"

"Hardly," Lucifer replied, "but Dave was just about to take us to see little Timmy."

The woman's eyes bulged as she grabbed a nearby lamp and held it like a bat. Woman growled as she swung the light fixture at Lucifer, "Over my dead body! I won't let you near my children!"

The lamp struck the fallen angel on the side of his head. He didn't flinch from the blow but when she swung again, her husband intervened, "Connie, stop!"

Connie glared at him, feeling betrayed by his actions. She was confused when all she saw in Dave's eyes was fear. "What the hell is wrong with you? They want our children!"

He pointed at his shotgun with a shaky hand as Lucifer coldly remarked, "Hell is an appropriate term here, Connie, but I must correct you. We're here to see Timmy and grant his Christmas wish."

Connie had a look of shock when her eyes saw her husband's shotgun. She stood frozen in place, clutching Dave as Lucifer and the she-devil pushed by the couple. The fallen angel walked into the living room and merrily called out, "Timmy Jones? Step forward, please."

Three children were sitting by the fireplace, drinking hot chocolate and looking at the two strangers. They all went silent as Lucifer held out the envelope and said, "I have a letter written to me and now I'm here to grant your Christmas wish, Timmy."

"Santa?" Timmy said with a timid voice.

"Almost, kid. Now, let's see what little Timmy wished for, shall we?" The fallen angel replied as he magically moved a chair over to him to sit on.

All the children eyed him with awe as he opened up the envelope and pulled out the letter. Paroxysm leaned on the back of the chair, reading over his shoulder and smiled.

Lucifer looked at her, which caused the she-devil to grin even more. He rolled his eyes as he read the letter and announced, "So, little Timmy wants a puppy because he loves them and wants one to cuddle with at night?" He glanced up at the boy and added, "Why not ask your parents for one?"

Dave and Connie rushed over and held onto Timmy when they saw him moving towards Lucifer. The little boy gulped as the fallen angel's eyes locked with his. He shifted from foot to foot nervously before saying, "Mommy and daddy said that I'm too young for one. I'm not 'sponcible enough yet."

"Well," Lucifer said as he eyed the trembling parents, "I'm not going to leave here without granting your wish, child."

The ruler of Hell motioned with his hand and, out of nowhere, a small four-legged creature appeared. Its fur was jet black and in spots on its back was a thick leathery hide. Its face looked deformed and it had two small horns next to its floppy ears.

The paws were large and had razor sharp talons. It wagged its stubby tail as Lucifer reached down and scratched its head as he spoke to it in Enochian.

Connie made a face as she blurted out, "What is that *thing*? It's so hideous!"

The fallen angel scoffed, as though offended, "Dear me. You act as if you've never seen a hellhound before. I handpicked this one from one of the best breeds in Hell and that's all you have to say? It's way better than the mongrels roaming the Earth. Don't fret, he's housebroken." As the puppy ran around the living room, it peed in various spots, which the ruler of Hell shrugged and added, "For the most part."

Lucifer motioned to the boy with a grin, "Come here and say hello to your new *puppy*!"

Timmy walked towards the deformed beast, but his parents grabbed him.

Paroxysm bared her razor-sharp teeth and threatened, "Release the child or I'll make you. I beg you, keep restraining him and see what happens when you cross Lucifer's orders. We won't hurt him, you have our word."

The parents reluctantly let Timmy go. The boy walked forward as his siblings looked on from behind their parents. He stuck his hand out for the little hellhound to sniff but to everyone's surprise, it spoke, "No need to do that," its voice was gruff and scratchy, "I'm yours to do whatever you want. I'll protect you from any that tries to cause you harm."

"A talking puppy!" Timmy's two brothers shouted as they ran from behind their stunned parents. Little hands were petting and stroking the little beast. One of Timmy's siblings asked Lucifer as he stood up, "Can I get a talking puppy too?"

"Did you write Satan a Christmas letter?"

"No," the boy pouted.

"Then you have your answer. Maybe the jolly fat man will get you some lovely toys, but he can't grant what I can."

"I'm going to enter – " Timmy announced, but then he stopped. He looked at the hellhound and asked, "Do you have a name?"

"What name do you want to call me by, Timmy?" The hellhound answered.

"Hmmm, I think that I'll name you Buster."

"Then henceforth, my name shall be Buster," the little deformed beast stated as it wagged its stubby tail.

Timmy excitedly stated, "I'm going to enter Buster in all those fancy dog shows and win blue ribbons for sure!"

The hellhound's red eyes pulsated as it commented, "If blue ribbons are what you desire, I'll gladly eat the other contestants in the show. This, I vow to you, if it pleases the Timmy."

Lucifer only shrugged at the family as he created a portal, "Do ensure that he's well fed or people *will go* missing. Raw meat will suffice. Take care and Merry Christmas!"

Paroxysm pulled out an envelope from his pocket and gave it to the fallen angel. He tweaked the portal and the two denizens from Hell stepped through, leaving the parents horrified with their mouths gaping open as the children played with their new *puppy*.

Chapter Eight

Star Wars, Sort Of

Lucifer walked out of the portal and was greeted by the sight of a luxurious neighborhood. All the lawns were immaculately trimmed and manicured. Every single driveway had multiple vehicles on them; each one probably cost a fourth of what the houses were worth.

Paroxysm noticed that there were security cameras throughout the neighborhood; every other lamp post had them attached to them. Lucifer glanced down the street and saw a car slowly driving their way. As the driver got closer, he turned on the spotlight on the side mirror and shined it on them.

The passenger door opened and a portly man in a security uniform stepped out. He strolled towards the intruders with his meaty fingers touching the handle of his gun and demanded, "Excuse me, but who are you and why are you here?"

"That's what Mankind has pondered throughout the centuries," Lucifer replied with a smirk.

"No time for games," the security guard said with frustration, "This is a private community. One that you don't belong in, so I'm going to have to ask you to leave or I'll have you both arrested!"

"I'm sure that you will try," the fallen angel said as he turned to find his next delivery, "but I'm on a tight schedule and can't be bothered by a mortal's perceived power of authority. Come along, Paroxysm–"

"Freeze!" The driver stepped out of the vehicle, brandishing his taser gun at them, "Either of you so much as take one more step and I'll light you up like a festive tree!"

Lucifer glared at the man, his eyes brightly glowing white, "Mind your tongue, *cretin*, or I'll show you exactly why I'm known as the *Lightbringer*."

The man froze but managed to fire his taser, striking Lucifer on his chest. He glanced down at the leads, as if bored, and said, "And now, it's my turn."

The fallen angel magically forced the leads off his chest, causing them to strike the security guard. The man fell down on the street, convulsing as the taser seemed more charged than it should be. His partner ran over to assist him, but Lucifer stepped in front of him. The portly guard reached for his gun, but the fallen angel hit him in the chest so hard that the security guard flew across the street. The man struck an iron fence, significantly denting it. The portly guard dropped down on the sidewalk unconscious.

Paroxysm smirked as she walked over to the tased guard, "Saw that coming."

She bent down and yanked the leads off the downed man. The she-devil leaned in and kissed him as she remarked before he died, "This is what happens when you interfere with Hell's will. You get burned in the end. See you soon."

Lucifer rolled his shoulders and adjusted his jacket and vest as he walked over to the sidewalk. He held the envelope and searched for the house in question, but then chuckled.

The she-devil glanced at him and asked, "Did you locate the next child?"

"I was trying to determine that from the magic, but then it occurred to me," the fallen angel replied with a grin as he turned the envelope in his hand, "If all else fails, look at the address. At least this one has it, albeit crudely written but decipherable."

"I'm surprised that it wasn't better. With all these expensive houses, you would think that the parents would have one of their minions do it for the urchin." The she-devil commented.

"If that were the case," Lucifer pointed out as they walked in tandem, "I doubt that the letter would have made it down to me but who knows."

Lucifer zeroed in on an extravagant house that had more Christmas lights and decorations on and around the property than most of the other houses. The two-story domicile looked like a mansion in its sheer size. The top floor had a dozen windows and each one looked like bedrooms. Each room appeared to have its own Christmas tree inside it and a green holly wreath hung on top of each window frame.

The bottom floor had much bigger windows that, if the curtains were drawn back, one could see the entirety of the floor layout. The roof was covered with strands of multicolor lights and, in the center, was a huge cross lit up with white lights.

"Could these occupants be any more obnoxious?" The fallen angel said aloud.

"If it pleases you," Paroxysm said with a mischievous grin, "I can go up there and invert it for you, sire."

"You cheeky little she-devil," Lucifer said as he focused his magic, trying to find the child's room, "It depends on the parents but, for now, we have a job to do."

The ruler of Hell strolled up the long driveway and was greeted by two large pit bulls that were chained up to a post on the finely manicured yard. The dogs growled menacingly but as the pair approached, Paroxysm's face shifted, revealing her true devil face. Her black eyes glowed as she snarled and baring her vicious teeth and claws, arching her back and looking huge.

The pit bulls whimpered and whined as they backed down with their tails between their legs. The she-devil grinned as she said, "Wealth can buy a lot of things, but it can't afford the protection of Hell."

"They could, for the right offer," Lucifer replied with a sigh, "but that's the problem with the wealthy mortals. They believe that they are superior to everyone and everything that they can't see that their money can't prevent them from being on your torture table."

The fallen angel stepped up to the front door and turned the knob. He was surprised that it wasn't locked so he pushed the door open.

He glanced at Paroxysm and said, "Hubris at its best. A perfect example of the false sense of security that a gated community has to offer."

The duo stepped inside and went down a long hallway. It was both warm and inviting, but at the same time it gave off an air of a fake facade. Every piece of furniture was expensive, imported, and immaculately clean. Classical music filled the house, along with laughter from the adults and bickering from the children.

The she-devil looked at the ruler of Hell and snarked, "This ought to be a joyous visit with these sweet little angels."

"Now, now," Lucifer replied as the arguing continued unabated, "don't be lumping me and my kind in with these creatures. At least we didn't squabble over who should get what."

"Never crossed my mind. Except for, you know, that whole rebellion thing," Paroxysm chuckled.

The fallen angel huffed as he glared at his minion as they rounded the corner that led into a large living room. Several adults were sitting along a marble top bar, drinking wine and chatting with each other. The children were tugging on various toys like hyenas fighting over the last bits of a carcass.

Lucifer pulled out the letter and read it for a moment before announcing with a booming voice, "Chad Masterson! Where is Chad Masterson at?"

The room fell completely silent, only the sound of music playing. All eyes looked at the new *guests,* uncertainty grazed over their faces.

The fallen angel spoke once again, "Right, now which one of you *children* is Chad Masterson."

"Who wants to know?" A salt and pepper haired man asked sternly as he stepped up to Lucifer, his breath reeked of alcohol and candy.

"Obviously, I do." The fallen angel replied, grinning ear to ear, "You people enjoy making it difficult to get deliveries here, don't you? So, where's the little urchin at? I haven't got all night."

One child was about to speak, but the man growled, "I don't know who you or your trollop is over there so unless you have a damn good reason for breaking into our house, I suggest that you leave before I call the cops."

"See?" The ruler of Hell looked back at Paroxysm, "The large amount of digits in a bank account proves my point."

"And what does that remark supposed to mean," the man demanded as he jabbed his finger on Lucifer's chest.

"The more money a mortal has, the greater the notion of their self-importance is," Lucifer replied as his eyes glowed brightly, "Touch me again and I'll ensure that you won't have a festive holiday tonight. Step aside and let me talk to the owner of this letter."

The man cowered away, clutching a gold cross around his neck. Lucifer rolled his eyes as a young boy, who was no more than nine, stood up. The kid glanced at the other children and then at the adults before stepping forward.

"Chad Masterson, I presume?" The fallen angel flatly asked with little amusement.

"I'm Chad. What do you want?"

"I'm here because you wrote me your Christmas letter and now, I'm here to seal the deal," Lucifer replied as he handed the boy the letter.

One of the older boys chortled, "You wrote a letter to Santa Claus? You're such a baby! You do realize that all our gifts come from Mom and Dad and our relatives?"

"Shut up, Jered!" Chad hissed, "Don't you think that I know that?"

"He doesn't look like Santa to me," a little girl hesitantly said as she peaked out from behind Jered.

"You're such a loser!" Another kid mocked, "Wait until I tell the other kids at school!"

"You're correct, little girl. I'm not the jolly old poster child for diabetes," the ruler of Hell stated as he slowly walked around, "Young Chad here didn't write Santa on the envelope, so I got it and now I'm here to present to you the gift that you asked for. Hands out, child."

Chad did as he was asked, excitement brightened the boy's face. Lucifer smiled as he sat the gift in the child's hands and said, "There you go."

Chad looked puzzled at it and then asked, "What exactly is this?"

"It's what you requested. It's a light saber. Unsheathe it and you'll be able to feel how light and balanced it is. A truly remarkable piece of craftsmanship." The fallen angel jovially replied.

Chad threw the weapon back at Lucifer, striking him in the chest, and angrily spat, "That's *not* what I asked for! I asked for a damn lightsaber, not a fucking sword!"

Lucifer sneered as his ire grew, "I'm starting to have a real disliking for this holiday. You asked for the weapon and yet, you have the audacity to spurn it? Tell me, boy, why shouldn't I smite this entire community?"

Paroxysm placed her hand on the fallen angel's shoulder and asked Chad, "Were you referring to the laser sword in those Star Wars movies?"

"The what?" The ruler of Hell said, feeling confused.

"Star Wars. It's that series of space fantasy movies and TV shows, sire." The she-devil informed her master.

Lucifer smiled fondly, "Ah yes. I do recall whispering in Lucas' ear about selling his franchise to Disney. The perfect form of chaos that has been festering with its fanbase ever since then. And you expect one of those weapons, Chad?"

"Duh!" The boy replied with exasperation, "How can this *dimwit* not know that?"

Lucifer leaned down, getting into Chad's face. His eyes glowing white as his wings appeared, causing everyone to cower, "I'll be right back, *whelp*!"

The ruler of Hell abruptly disappeared, leaving the she-devil alone with the people. She flashed her razor-sharp teeth at them as she said, "It's never wise to spurn a gift, especially from Lucifer himself. I wouldn't be surprised if he levels this snobbish, piss-posh neighborhood. Just know that if he does, I'll be seeing *all* of you shortly."

"Whatever," Chad brazenly brushed off the threat, "He's the idiot that doesn't know what I asked for. I asked for a lightsaber and that's what I want. I *always* get what I want!"

"Keep quiet, boy!" One of the adults admonished, "Don't you know who you were talking to?"

"Like they can do anything to me," Chad retorted as he stepped up in front of the she-devil. The boy smugly boasted, "It's a deal that *he* has to make good on. I made a request and Satan replied by showing up, thus making him obligated to fulfill my request. Isn't that right, *lackey*?"

Paroxysm malevolently smiled at the child as she stroked her fingers along his cheek, "My dear boy. You don't get it, do you? Lucifer doesn't follow the laws and rules of humanity. When you make a deal with the Devil, be prepared to pay the price. Lucifer doesn't take insolence nicely so I suggest that you stow that entitled attitude, if you know what's good for you."

At that moment, Lucifer reappeared. Chad looked at the fallen angel and snarked, "Well? Do you have *my* lightsaber or not?"

"Not the one that you requested because it doesn't exist in reality, but I did bring a weapon comparable to it." The ruler of Hell replied with contempt as he towered over the boy. Before Chad could speak, the fallen angel pulled out a sword, the blade glowed a bright orange as if it had been pulled out of a forge.

The boy was so enamored by it that he reached out to touch the blade. Lucifer smacked his hand away and said, "I don't advise you to touch it, unless you want to lose your fingers. This sword has been forged in the fires of Hell and will cut through anything and can immolate things upon touching it. It may not be your mythical weapon, but it's the best you're going to get."

Chad and the other children seemed in awe of the weapon, but a woman shrieked, "You can't just give him that! He's just a child!"

"Like any of you buffoons truly care," the ruler of Hell replied as he handed the weapon to Chad, "If you did, this little ragamuffin wouldn't be as terrible as he is now. This weapon is yours, but it comes with a price."

"I'm not paying you for it! It's a damn gift!" Chad snarled as he grabbed the hilt and attempted to stab Lucifer. The fallen angel caught the blade with his hand, keeping the kid from moving it.

"It's not about money, child. The price is that whenever you choose to wield this sword, you will feel an irresistible pull to create mayhem and destruction. Any around you will suffer and possibly die on this blade. It all depends on you, Chad Masterson. I've fulfilled my end of this wish. What you do from here on out is on you and you alone." Lucifer released the sword from his grasp and added with a sneer, "Come along, Paroxysm. We're leaving."

As the duo turned around and walked away, Chad's face contorted and his blue eyes turned blood red. Paroxysm opened the front door and stepped outside, waiting for her master. Shouting and screaming rang out as Lucifer stepped outside.

He closed the door and broke the handle off like he was picking a daisy from the ground and said, "Like I said, wealth doesn't buy proper security. These folks shall soon discover that when little Chad Masterson goes on a little destructive spree through this gated community."

Smoke billowed out as the child came out the backdoor, touching his new *toy* on anything that he could burn. An eerie orange glow soon engulfed the tranquil community.

As Lucifer looked at the next envelope and opened a portal, Paroxysm shrugged her shoulders and replied, "Merry Christmas, you filthy animals."

Chapter Nine

My Little Hell-Pony

Lucifer stepped out of the portal and surveyed the area. The landscape was nothing more than rural flatlands that were sparsely covered with trees. Herds of cattle were huddled together for warmth in one of the pastures. There were only a handful of ranch-style houses here, each one had a minimal amount of Christmas decorations on them.

Lucifer spotted the house from their vantage point and slowly walked towards it. It sat off the dirt road and had a long, tire rut driveway with patches of packed grass in the middle. Paroxysm spotted a small pack of coyotes watching them.

She bared her razor-sharp teeth and menacingly growled in their direction. The pack yipped and whimpered as they scurried away.

"Having fun with the local beasts?" Lucifer asked.

"Somebody has to teach the mongrels who's on top of the pecking order here," the she-devil replied, still glaring at the retreating pack.

The fallen angel shook his head and chuckled, "Do you really think that my Father's animals here are an actual threat?"

"No," the she-devil replied with a grin, "but I do love creating fear. It's one of my few redeeming qualities that keeps me going."

Snow lightly fell as the duo approached a long metal gate. Lucifer scaled over it with ease. As he adjusted his white leather jacket and vest, a creaking noise caught his attention. Paroxysm had opened the gate just wide enough to slip through.

She closed and locked it back in place, looked at the fallen angel and asked, "What?"

"You could have told me that you knew how to do that," Lucifer stated with irritation.

The she-devil responded with amusement, "You didn't give me a chance to say anything. You hopped over it but I didn't feel like exerting myself like that. Besides, the cold metal would have been too frosty on my devilish bits if I straddled it."

The farmhouse seemed well kept, the smell of fresh coats of paint was prominent as the dirt road gave way to white gravel. Paroxysm noted the stables were empty and cleaned out. No signs of any livestock were present.

"Do you think these people only grow food?" The she-devil asked.

"I can't say. There's too much snow covering the land to say for certain. Why do you ask?"

Paroxysm pointed, "Immaculate stables but no livestock. I'm just curious as to what these people do."

Lucifer shrugged his shoulders as they got to a slab of concrete that was used as a porch, "I don't know and I don't care. Perhaps they just bought the place and can't afford those luxuries. We're here for the child, nothing more."

The fallen angel used his magic to unlock the front door and then noticed that the she-devil's brow was furrowed and kept looking around. He turned to her and asked, "What is it?"

"I don't know, sire," Paroxysm replied as she kept looking around, "Something about this place feels…off. Can't you sense it, sire?"

"The only thing that I sense is that we're running out of time for this holiday," Lucifer said as he quietly opened the door. As he stuck his head in, the fallen angel backed up. He glanced at the she-devil and asked, "Step inside and let me know if what you're feeling is coming from within."

She nodded as she warily pushed past the ruler of Hell and into the house. Paroxysm slowly looked around before turning to her master and stating, "It feels different, like it's more inviting in here. Not like outside."

Lucifer pointed out the door as he fully entered the space, "Then go out and find the source. I'm getting the sense that we're being watched. I suspect that our movements have attracted an audience."

Paroxysm snarled as she rushed back outside, leaving Lucifer on his own. He surveyed the living room that connected directly with an open kitchen as he strolled around, seeing a bunch of holiday decorations and religious sayings on each wall. He paused by one that read *Godliness is next to cleanliness*.

He ran a finger over the frame and chuckled when his finger came away with dust, "Hardly accurate. Someone needs to practice what they preach here."

The fallen angel wiped his hands as he used the piece of mail to find its owner. He walked down a long hallway that was covered in more religious items and family pictures. Lucifer reached the last door on his left, next to a beaten-up closet door that housed an older model water heater.

The door was slightly ajar so he gently pushed it open. The bedroom was lit up from the ambient light from several nightlights. Each of the paneling-covered walls had small, painted wooden shelves screwed into them. Posters decorated most of the void space with one subject: horses, from running wild in a meadow up to being ridden in a race.

The child, who couldn't be no more than seven years ago, constantly shifted on her small bed. It too had the equestrian theme on the blanket and pillow cases. The little blonde girl rolled over, clutching a stuffed horse in her tiny arms. Lucifer nudged the bed with his foot several times, rousing the child from her restless sleep.

"What?" The little girl whined, still half asleep, "I'm not ready to go to school."

"Lucky for you, that's not why I'm waking you up," the fallen angel replied as he sat down on the only seat in the bedroom.

The little girl sat up, not recognizing the voice. She reached over and turned her equestrian lamp on and saw the fallen angel. Lucifer was slowly rocking back and forth on a wooden rocking horse, smiling ear to ear.

"Who are you, mister, and why are you here?" The child asked as she grabbed a food-encrusted butter knife off a plate that had a partially eaten sandwich on her nightstand.

"I'm making my rounds on this joyous holiday night," Lucifer replied as he waved one arm up in the air, like he was trying to tame a wild stallion, "You're Amy Riggs, correct?"

"Yes, I am, but who are you and why are you in my room?" Amy asked, still pointing the butter knife at the fallen angel.

Lucifer pulled out an envelope from his jacket pocket and showed the equestrian theme envelope to her and asked, "Is this your letter that you wrote to me, child?"

"Oh my God! You actually got my wish?" Amy replied with surprise.

Lucifer raised an eyebrow and said, "There's no need in bringing my Father into this conversation. Wait a moment, are you saying that you actually wrote this letter to me?"

Amy shook her head with excitement as she sat up on the side of her bed, "Of course I did! Why wouldn't I since Santa isn't looking to answer my letters lately."

Lucifer turned the envelope over and looked at it. He could see that the writing on it was legible and easy to read.

The fallen angel looked back at Amy and asked, "With all the religious apparel in your quaint domicile, why turn to me? Don't you realize who you're addressing?"

"Yes, my only hope," Amy replied as her little shoulders sagged.

"What's wrong, little one? Why are you so desperate for my help with a Christmas present?" The ruler of Hell asked, noting that her excitement quickly evaporated and morphed in melancholy.

"Read the letter and hopefully you'll understand," Amy answered as she looked down at the floor.

Lucifer sighed but did as the little blonde girl asked. He pulled out the letter and quietly read it to himself.

Dear Satan,

I'm not sure how things work with you. I know that I shouldn't be doing this but my family is in bad shape. I overheard my parents saying that if we can't bring in more income, we will lose the ranch. I want to help out but I'm too young to work a normal kind of job. I'm asking for a horse that I can ride in the rodeo circuit and other competitions. Unfortunately, my parents can't afford one for me, let alone its upkeep. If I had a horse, I could at least contribute and not have to wonder if we will lose everything.

Thanks for reading this,

Amy Riggs.

Lucifer looked up at the little girl for a moment and then said, "So, your answer to everything is a horse?"

Amy nodded but didn't look at the fallen angel, "Yes sir. I'm a great rider for my age. I don't have anything to give you, other than my soul."

"Please, don't get all melodramatic about this," the fallen angel said as he stood up, towering over the child, "That's not what I do and I'm not handing out Christmas gifts in exchange for the souls of children."

Amy looked up at the fallen angel with confusion, "But I thought–"

Lucifer held up his hand and cut her off, "I don't do most of the things that you have been told. I do tempt humans because I know that they will succumb to whatever desires resides in their hearts. I don't have good people tortured in Hell, just the bad ones that truly deserve punishment." The fallen angel reached out and picked up an old, leather-bound Bible and added, "Don't go putting much stock in this book. It may have the words of my Father in it, but humanity has twisted its meaning and changed the narrative to hold power over others. You're better off doing your own search for knowledge rather than relying on this alone."

"Are you saying that I shouldn't read the Bible?" Amy asked.

Lucifer handed the Bible to Amy and said, "I honestly don't care what you do, child. Read it, if it pleases you, but know that you'd be better off thinking for yourself. That said, I believe that it's time to make your Christmas wish a reality. So, bundle up. It's a bit frosty outside."

Amy brightly smiled as she looked at the ruler of Hell. She hopped off her bed and scurried over to her closet as Lucifer stepped out of the room. He strolled towards the front door with his hands behind his back, patiently waiting. The fallen angel closed his eyes, sensing a familiar presence nearby.

Lucifer wasn't sure who or what was outside, but one thing he knew for certain: no one was going to prevent him from delivering these gifts tonight.

Amy walked towards the fallen angel grinning and giddy with excitement.

He held out his hand and said, "Come along, Amy."

They walked out into the cold, snowy night, heading towards an old stable in need of some serious restoration. Lucifer casually glanced around, trying to locate the source of the interloper. He could feel that Paroxysm was near it, possibly fighting with it.

As they stood before the stable, the ruler of Hell announced as he clapped his hands, "Right. One wish, coming up."

A hazy, orange rift tore open before them, the heat emanating from it created a steamy fog around it from intermingling with cold, winter weather. The rift glowed brightly as a creature burst through it.

The beast looked like a horse, only much bigger and had crimson veins covering its body that would pulsate with each breath it took. The eyes were jet black with, what looked like to the little girl, a dancing flame in center.

"Whoa," Amy said as she looked at the beast as it stamped its fiery hoof on the snowy ground, melting it as flames made contact with each strike. "What is that?"

Lucifer stroked his hand along the horse's long neck and said, "This is known as a hell horse. Beautiful, isn't she?"

"Yes and," Amy gulped, "scary looking too."

"You're seeing her in her true form because you are open to seeing such things," Lucifer explained as he knelt down next to Amy, "Don't worry. No one else can see her like this unless she allows it. To everyone, this marvelous creature will only catch their attention as she easily makes it to the winner's circle."

"What about the flames? Will it set everything on fire?" Amy asked as she pointed at the hooves.

"Not unless she wants to. It will appear to be dust and dirt being kicked up. Now, reach out your hand and introduce yourself to her." The fallen angel instructed.

Amy tentatively reached out a shaky hand, feeling a little frightened by the beast. The hell horse leaned its head down, snorting several times before rubbing its snout against her soft hand.

"Ah, she likes you, Amy. That's a good sign." Lucifer said before he put a hand on the hell horse's forehead and commanded, "You are now bonded to Amy Riggs. You will help her with whatever she needs you to do and protect her from harm. Do you understand this?"

The hell horse slowly nodded as its gaze fell on the little girl. The ruler of Hell looked over at Amy and said, "She requires a name.

She has one but it's not easy to say in your native tongue."

Amy thought about it for a moment and then said, "Flickers, like the fire in her eyes. What does she eat? My parents might not allow me to keep her."

"Flickers can graze on her own. She doesn't need much, food wise, because she can fend for herself." Lucifer answered but as Amy was about to speak, he added, "Trust me when I say, you don't want to know what she eats. As for your parents, we can talk to them now."

Amy turned around and saw her parents running towards them. Her father had a double barrel shotgun in his hands and had on a white shirt and pajama pants as his bathrobe flapped in the wind. The mother had a long, brown duster that mostly covered her pink nightgown and had an iron poker as her weapon of choice.

The man raised the shotgun and demanded, "Get away from my daughter! Amy, come over here now!"

"Has this strange man hurt you?" The mother asked as she glared at the ruler of Hell.

"No, momma. He's giving me this horse for Christmas! Isn't that great!" Amy cried out as she joyfully ran over to her parents. She turned around and said, "I love her! Thanks, Lucifer!"

"My pleasure, child," the fallen angel said as he walked up to the family.

The father aimed the shotgun at Lucifer's chest as he cocked the hammer back and ordered, "Stay right where you are! You come any closer, I won't hesitate to shoot you!"

"But daddy," Amy pleaded, "I asked Lucifer to come here tonight. I wanted a horse and he gave it to me. Don't shoot him."

"Amy, love," the mother said as she held her child, "you know that we can't afford this animal. We simply don't have the money for it." She looked up at the ruler of Hell and said, "I'm sorry, mister, but you need to take your horse back."

"I can't. Flickers has already bonded with the child. Fear not, the horse can tend to its own needs, just give her some grooming and a good ride now and then." Lucifer replied.

"I don't think you heard my wife." The father threatened as he put a finger on the trigger, "It's not a request, take the beast with you. It can't stay here!"

"Not my concern. I granted Amy her wish and I'm a Devil of my word. Even if I took Flickers back down to Hell, she would make her way back up here."

The husband laughed, not believing the ruler of Hell, "Are you actually suggesting that you're the Devil himself? I find that hard to believe."

"No really, daddy. He's truly the Devil," Amy spoke up, "I wrote a Christmas letter to him and Lucifer brought me my own horse so that I-"

"That's enough of this foolishness." The man angrily cut off his daughter, "The man is crazy and needs to be locked up for his own good! So, tell me, *Lucifer,* which pasture did you steal the horse from? Maggie, go call the sheriff."

Lucifer sighed, "I don't have time for any of this nonsense. I suppose a demonstration is in order."

The fallen angel's eyes brightly glowed white as he let his tendril wings unfurrow as he lifted up in the air. The hell horse snorted and let out a guttural growl as it raised up on its hind legs, showing its true form as fire danced on its hooves. The little flame in the hell horse's eyes engulfed the black orbs. Its incisors transformed into deadly, razor-sharp teeth similar to a shark.

The family cowered as the ruler of Hell left them. Lucifer flew over to the area where he felt Paroxysm was at and saw that she had one of his brethren pinned down on the ground.

Lucifer landed near the scuffle and said with a jovial laugh, "Well if it isn't Raguel. I wasn't expecting to see you out tonight. What brings you to this quaint slice of Earth?"

"You, Lucifer!" The angel replied as he thrashed around, trying to free himself from Paroxysm's grip. "You shouldn't be up here. You belong in Hell where Father cast you!"

"Can I kill him now or shall I wait for you to interrogate this interloper, sire?" The she-devil asked.

"You can't kill me, *abomination*!" Raguel defiantly retorted, "None of your weapons can slay an angel of the Lord!"

"Ooh, he's a feisty one! Can I keep him to play with in Hell? I promise to walk him and feed him every day." The she-devil asked with a coy smile as she ran her fingers through Raguel's gray hair

The fallen angel pinched the bridge of his nose, "Let him go, Paroxysm. I'd like to hear what the angel of Justice and Harmony has to say."

Paroxysm let the angel go as she pouted, "Fine, my lord, but he would've made a great tree topper in my chamber."

Raguel stood up and glared at the she-devil as she walked over to Lucifer. He adjusted his silver robes that covered his charcoal armor and proclaimed, "You have been found guilty of creating a lot of chaos tonight. All of your hell spawn has been disrupting the harmony of Father's world. What do you have to say for yourself before I pass judgment upon you?"

"Clearly, you've already judged me, much like you did eons ago," Lucifer replied as he pulled out an envelope, "I'm guilty as charged but, in my defense, I had this thrust upon me."

"What does that mean, Lucifer?" Raguel asked as he squinted his eyes with suspicion, "No one can make archangels do anything against their will. Why should I believe your claim? You're a liar and a deceiver."

"Persuasive player of one's desires," Lucifer corrected Raguel as he handed the envelope over to the angel, "I'm not a liar, but I do have a great influence over what humans want. It's in their nature to want the forbidden fruit. I merely nudge them in that direction. Tonight, however, I was challenged to partake in this holiday by a trickster."

"Hmm," Raguel inspected the envelope closely, reading the word Satan on it in red crayon, "So you say that this trickster went down to Hell and threw down the gauntlet of merriment at your feet? I don't see how that's possible."

"This Rabbit managed to magically pierce my realm with a sack load of children's letters addressed to me, asking for gifts. It's a deal, Raguel. You know as well as myself that I can't say no to those bargaining with the Devil."

Raguel smirked, "Much like that famous fiddle contest?"

Lucifer huffed in frustration, "Why must you bring that up? I challenged him and the hillbilly won. Same principle here. I must deliver the gifts to the children tonight."

"But why have your demonic creatures aid in the delivery?" The angel of Justice and Harmony asked.

"Unlike the jolly fat man, who can do this holiday in one night, I can't." Lucifer begrudgingly admitted, much to his dismay, "Unlike Santa, I have to use my minions or the children won't get what they asked for. Is that so wrong?"

"It is when they go roaming the Earth slaughtering people," the angel stated with a knowing look. "There are people on the streets all over the world that have been possessed by demons! Are you planning an insurrection on Father's creation? If so, more innocent lives will perish."

Lucifer took a moment and focused on the accusations, then he smiled, "They were doing what was asked of them in the wish. Little Bradley asked that all the mean people stop fighting and have world peace. That's not such a bad tradeoff? Little Reba felt bad seeing all the homeless people freezing so my demons are inhabiting their bodies so they won't succumb to the frigid weather. Is that a terrible crime?"

"You are right, but the power vacuum left in the wake of all the deaths of these politicians and warmongers will create discord for a long time. Who's to say that others won't come in to make things worse on our Father's creation?" Raguel countered.

The ruler of Hell shrugged his shoulders, "Humanity has that nasty habit, don't they? Should I summon Purah to resurrect the dead? From what I understand, she's currently shacking up with a demigod these days in one of our Father's broken multiverses of this world. Nice fellow. Duncan, his name is. Don't fret, I'll punish the culprits that's causing you such grief, brother."

"I've already smote them. Before they died, they told me that you were here on Earth." Raguel said as he handed Lucifer the envelope back, "I thought that they were lying about your presence here, but I see that even demons can be honest."

The fallen angel stuck it back into his jacket pocket and cheerfully said, "Good. Now that you sorted it out, I must be going. I still have a few more gifts to deliver."

"You still need to atone for all this chaos you created! " the angel responded as he pointed an accusatory finger at the ruler of Hell. "What about the possessed humans?"

Lucifer created a portal to the next location and said, "The homeless will be given the choice of remaining possessed or not. It's only fair since my minions are keeping them alive and safe. I counter your accusations with this: am I the one truly responsible for this mess or is it this trickster? My minions are scouring the world for the trickster as we speak. I've also put out a sizable bounty on it as well. If you want, try and find it. You held the envelope so you have its magical signature. Whoever does can punish Rabbit for its transgressions that occurred tonight."

"I'm sure that I'll find this Rabbit before your lowly minions do," Raguel smugly remarked.

"May the best archangel win. Come along, Paroxysm," Lucifer said as the two walked through the portal to their next stop.

Chapter Ten

Raggedy Ann

They stepped out on the roof of a high-rise building. The aroma of freshly-laid tar and pigeon droppings saturated the air. Lucifer walked over to the ledge and surveyed the sprawling metropolis.

"New York. Definitely a place filled to the brim with violence and strong opinionated people." Lucifer said with a smile.

"Yes, sire. It does sound like a lovely place." Paroxysm commented as she stood next to the fallen angel.

"Feeling homesick yet?" The ruler of Hell asked as he observed several men assaulting a young man in the alley next to the building.

"I'd be lying if I said no," the she-devil answered. "Earth is a lovely place to visit, but it isn't home. At least in Hell, people know their place."

Lucifer nodded in agreement as he turned around. He strolled to the rooftop door and opened it. The stairwell felt damp with the telltale aroma of freshly painted walls, the steel steps were sticky with each footfall.

Paroxysm ran her claws along the railing, causing sparks to fly. Lucifer wondered if all this was worth it. He already had a confrontation with the Angel of Justice and Harmony and now the fallen angel was curious if any of his other brothers and sisters would interfere with his gift-giving.

I don't like this, but what choice do I have, Lucifer mentally mused?

The click-clacking of their footfalls echoed loudly within the stairwell as the duo from Hell descended. Once they reached the 33rd floor landing, the ruler of Hell opened the side door and stepped inside.

The hallway was lined with a plush, burgundy carpet with long, runner rugs that had yellow, red, and blue geometric patterns. The walls were painted beige and had dark wooden trimming along the middle.

Ornate light fixtures dangled from the ceiling from shiny golden chains. There were wreaths on all the apartment doors adorned with red ribbons, gold and silver tensile, and fake holly berries. Right below them were festively decorated stockings, bulging with candies and other gifts.

Lucifer paused next to a door that shiny blue garland lining the trimming with the numbers 3366. He placed his hand on the doorknob and turned it but the door didn't budge.

He focused his angelic magic on the locking mechanism and said, "I don't know about you but I'm ready to be done with these deliveries."

"As lovely as this little excursion has been," Paroxysm replied as she straightened out her outfit, "it doesn't compare to Hell. I do miss the constant wailings from all the damned souls."

"If you're in need to torture someone," the ruler of Hell stated as the tumblers clicked into place, unlocking the door, "you can pop out of here for a bit. You wouldn't have to go far to find people that deserve to be punished here in this city."

"It's not the same, sire," the she-devil answered as they stepped into the apartment. "Don't get me wrong. It's quite fun bathing in their blood but there's a difference between our realms. I don't feel the magical connection that I have down in Hell. Plus, I miss my pain parlor and all my torturous devices."

The apartment was spacious with an open floor plan. It had hardwood flooring and a modern design theme of black, gray, and white furniture and appliances. Along the outer wall were floor to ceiling windows with a breathtaking view of the bustling city.

Paroxysm walked over to the refrigerator and opened the door. She chuckled as she pulled out a covered tray and said, "Look, sire. They have your eggs! Isn't that thoughtful?"

Lucifer furrowed his brow as he replied flatly, "Really? Of all the foods you could eat in that refrigerator and *those* chicken butt nuggets gets you excited?"

The she-devil tossed the tinfoil cover off and snatched several eggs and stuffed them in her mouth as she replied with an eggy grin, "Of course! Think of these as tribute to your greatness. Now, if only they had some devil's food cake, it would be a perfect meal."

The ruler of Hell rolled his eyes and said with exasperation, "And how would some confectioner's creation make it perfect?"

Paroxysm wiggled her eyebrows suggestively, "They're both *sinfully* delightful, sire."

Lucifer rolled his eyes and sighed as the she-devil stabbed her claws into the eggs like shish kabobs and told her, "Eat up then. I'm going to go see the little urchin and give my gift so be on our merry way. Try not to make a huge mess."

The ruler of Hell marched across the open living room to a door that had colorful, hand-drawn art adoring it. A small sign hung on the door that read: *This is a God worshiping house. No sin in our den.*

"Oh, please," Lucifer muttered as he opened the door and slipped inside quietly.

The child's room was sparsely decorated with more artwork, each had glitter that sparkled under the ambient light of nightlights that were plugged into electrical outlets.

The floor was free of debris, something that the fallen angel hadn't seen in a child's room. No toys were strewn about nor any remnants of old, partially eaten foods.

It appeared immaculate.

A large chest in the corner of the room had numerous dolls, ranging from porcelain to plastic, that were threatening to spill out. Other than that, the child kept her room tidy. Something felt off to Lucifer, which had him puzzled and concerned. He quietly walked around the room, noting that there wasn't a speck of dust anywhere to be found.

Either this little girl is a neat freak or something else is at play, the ruler of Hell mused.

Lucifer thought about the appearance of this domicile and realized that it too was in pristine condition and showed no signs of children living here. He turned around and crept out of the child's room and methodically observed the apartment.

Paroxysm watched her master walking around, inspecting everything and asked, "Is something wrong, sire?"

"I'm not entirely sure at the moment but something about this place feels off." Lucifer replied with a puzzled visage.

Concern etched on her visage, the she-devil asked, "Did you make your delivery yet? What can I do to help, sire?"

"Not yet but I'm feeling…worried," Lucifer said. He looked at his minion and added, "Use your skills as a torturer and ferret out the root of this, Paroxysm."

"Do you believe that it has something to do with the religious apparel here?" The she-devil asked as she walked over to a wall that was adorned with several crosses and had few picture frames with biblical scriptures in them.

"Possibly, but I won't know until I talk with the little one," Lucifer replied as he turned around and went back into the child's room. He closed the door quietly behind him and noticed that the little girl was sitting up on her bed, looking at him.

She appeared disheveled as she clutched her blanket to her small body, "Are...are you here for me?" The child asked, fear laced in her voice.

Lucifer pulled out the envelope and said, "Is your name Jenny Davis?" When the child slowly nodded, he smiled brightly as he continued to say, "Splendid! I received your Christmas wish and I'm here to grant it!"

"Oh," Jenny said flatly. "I thought that I brought you here to take me."

Lucifer cocked his head to the side, eyeing her as he asked, "What *exactly* do you mean by that? In a way, you did summon me here because of this letter but I'm only dropping off, not picking up."

"But sir," Jenny said, not wanting to look at the ruler of Hell directly, "my parents said that one day you would take me down to Hell to be tortured and burned alive."

The fallen angel gasped, causing Jenny to look at him. She was surprised to see that he genuinely looked astonished.

Lucifer sat down on the edge of the bed and asked, "I don't do that sort of thing, my dear. I have my minions punish the souls of the wicked for their transgressions for as long as I need them to. Why on Earth would your parents be filling your head with this nonsense?"

Jenny looked down at the floor as a single tear trickled down her face. Lucifer sat in silence, feeling both confused and enraged.

After a couple of minutes of silence, the child finally said, "I'm different."

"What's wrong with being different, Jenny? It's not a crime to be different and it certainly doesn't get you sent down to my realm."

"But sir, I— "

"Please, call me Lucifer." The fallen angel interrupted her with a beguiling smile.

"Lucifer," Jenny said as she fidgeted with her hands, "I'm *different*. My parents say that I'm an abomination in the eyes of God. That I shouldn't exist. I'm broken and should have died at birth."

Lucifer furrowed his brow, looking down at the floor with her, "What kind of parents are these people? You look fine to me. How would they *presume* to know what dear old Dad would think about you?"

The child got up and stood before the fallen angel. Jenny tugged her nightshirt off and tossed it on the bed. She hugged her stomach and looked away in shame. Her white underwear was soiled with brown and crimson stains. Lucifer could see numerous bruises and scars, some fresh and others were old, covering her entire body.

Anger filled the ruler of Hell as he asked between gritted teeth, "Who's responsible for all of these, Jenny?"

Jenny shrugged her little shoulders and replied, "I am, sir—I mean Lucifer. It's what I rightfully deserve, according to my parents. It's the only way that God will accept me since I'm not normal."

"No child deserves this kind of treatment." Lucifer said, doing his best to quell his ire. "What exactly do you mean by not being normal?"

"I have parts here," Jenny said, pointing at her crotch, "that I'm not supposed to have. I'm a girl with boy parts. My parents said that I'm a girl and should only have girl parts, not both."

"I see." The ruler of Hell said as noises came from beyond the bedroom door, along with shouting and cursing. Lucifer grabbed the nightshirt and tossed it to Jenny and ordered, "Get dressed and stay in here. I'm going to have a little chat with your parents."

Jenny panicked as she cried out, "Please don't! That will only make things worse! I'll get a whipping for sure!"

"Not if I have a say in this matter." Lucifer reassured the child. "I'm going to have Paroxysm come in here and keep you safe. If either one of your parents comes in here, they'll have to get through her."

"But, I'm not worth it," Jenny replied as she slipped the nightshirt back on just as the fallen angel got to the door.

He placed his hand on the doorknob but before he turned it, Lucifer looked over his shoulder and said, "I may be viewed by people as evil incarnate, but there's one thing that I don't do and that's abuse children. No one deserves abuse in any form, certainly not a child. I punish those that deserve it and you, Jenny, are *not* on that list."

The fallen angel swung open the bedroom door and saw Paroxysm standing in front of Jenny's parents as they yelled at her.

The father pointed an accusatory finger at the she-devil as he exclaimed, "Filthy trollop! Get your slutty, scantily-clad ass out of our house or I'll call the cops!"

"You say that like I should be intimidated," Paroxysm replied, feeling amused, "You mortals always have an overinflated sense of control. You have no idea who you are threatening. I'd love to see you two try and make us leave."

"That's it! I'm calling the cops!" The woman exclaimed as she rushed over to grab a cordless phone on the wall.

As she dialed 911, Lucifer announced, "Please do that. I'm sure that the authorities would *love* to see how you've been treating little Jenny."

The woman paused as the operator answered the call. She glanced between her husband and the fallen angel before saying, "Yes, we need help. There are two intruders in our apartment. The Prominence Building, apartment 3366. Please hurry!"

The woman hung up the phone and rushed back over to her husband as he demanded, "Who the hell are you people and why are you in our home? Are you looking to rob us on this holy night?"

"Please," Lucifer scowled in disgust, "you two wouldn't know what holy is, even if it came down the chimney and bit you both on the ass. Paroxysm, be a dear and go be with little Jenny and keep her safe from these two buffoons."

The she-devil's black eyes glowed brightly as she glared at the parents as she asked, "Do you want me to *see* into her mind, sire?"

"If you wish," the fallen angel replied, not taking his steely gaze off Jenny's parents. "Protect her while I have a little chat with these two."

The she-devil nodded curtly as walked towards Jenny's bedroom. The father yelled at the duo, spittle spraying from his mouth, "You two leave our child alone! If either of you hurt her— "

Lucifer maniacally laughed, though there wasn't any humor in it as he cut off the man's tirade, "Hurt her? You two are doing a fine job at that without our help. I've seen your acts of cruelty that you've both inflicted on Jenny so I believe that it's high time for *both* of you to be punished."

"The police will be here any time now," the wife said as she pointed at the front door. "I suggest you leave now or you'll be put in jail."

"I don't fear your primitive incarcerations here." Lucifer retorted as his eyes brightly glowed white. "Do you really think that such cages can actually contain an archangel?"

"Stop your nonsense, you crazy bastard!" the husband shouted. "You don't scare us with this charade you're playing."

"You two should be more afraid of what Jenny will say to the police when they get here. I'm sure that God won't come down and shield you. He should smite the two of you for taking His name in vain."

"We would *never* take God's name in vain!" The woman protested, "This is a home that worships God. We would *never* break His laws!"

"If this is true," Lucifer challenged as he approached the couple, "then why do you hurt your daughter? Hypocrites! Sanctimonious moral judgment is what resides in this place, not my Father. You both hurt her because she was born different and use dear old Dad as a righteous shield to justify your ignorance and cruelty on an innocent child. *That's* taking God's name in vain."

The husband charged the ruler of Hell, screaming as his face reddened with rage. He punched Lucifer in the face and immediately crumpled on his knees, clutching his hand.

The man's wife rushed over to her husband, trying to comfort him as she hissed, "What the fuck did you do to him?"

"He punched me and broke his little hand on my face." Lucifer stated without a care. "Maybe next time he'll think twice about fighting the Devil."

"You're a devil," the man bit out as tears streamed down his sweat-soaked face, "but not the Devil! You're a madman and—"

Lucifer unfurled his wings before the couple, leaving them both speechless. He levitated in the air, his eyes glowing brightly as he proclaimed, "If this little demonstration doesn't convince you, then nothing ever will. You told Jenny that the Devil would come here and drag her to Hell on a daily basis that she actually believes you! Well, I'm here now and I'm not doing that, but I'd have no qualms taking you both in her stead. I came here to grant her Christmas wish. I should have my hellhounds tear you both apart! Your judgment day is at hand!"

The couple scooted away, cowering fearfully against the wall. Jenny's bedroom door opened as Paroxysm escorted the child. The she-devil glared at the parents, looking to tear them apart. Lucifer lowered himself back to the floor. He turned and looked at the she-devil and asked, "Why is Jenny out here?"

"She insisted," Paroxysm said as she stood protectively in front of the little girl, pointing a finger at the parents. "I'm inclined to kill them after what I saw in her head, sire."

"Killing them?" Lucifer tsked, "Paroxysm, you can come up with a better punishment than that. I need some alone time with Jenny to grant her wish. So, have fun with them and get creative."

"With pleasure," the she-devil answered as a diabolical smile spread across her visage.

Lucifer walked over to the little girl and ushered her back into her room. He closed the door and walked beside Jenny towards her bed. The fallen angel sat down on the side of her bed and pulled out the envelope and opened it.

As he read it to himself, Jenny asked, "Do you think that I actually deserve a present? I'm just a mistake and a blight against God."

"You do, Jenny and, for the record, how you're born doesn't offend my Father. Your parents are being cruel and don't deserve to raise a special child like you. That said, your letter to me says that you want a friend that can look past your *wrongness*, as you put it, and cares about you."

"Is-" Jenny asked hesitantly as she looked down at her hands as she fidgeted with them nervously, "is that too selfish of me to ask for that?"

Lucifer's lips parted slightly before he said, "Why would wanting a friend in this cruel world of my Father's be selfish, child?" He glanced at the door and added with a slight sneer, "Nevermind, I know exactly why you would think this way. I believe that I know how to grant your wish but you'll need to get ready first. You're leaving this dreadful place."

Jenny panicked, "Are you dragging me to Hell!?"

"What? No, Hell isn't a place for children, let alone make friends."

"Then where am I going, Mr Lucifer? Um...Will we all be going" The child asked tentatively, casting her gaze at her bedroom door.

Lucifer stood up and pointed at her toy chest and said, "I want you to pick out two of your least favorite dolls and hand them over to me."

Jenny slipped off the bed and padded over to the box. She tossed all the dolls on the floor but kept glancing at her door, expecting her parents to enter at any moment.

"Fear not, Jenny. They won't be coming in here. Paroxysm is keeping them *entertained*." Lucifer reassured her as he rubbed his hands together vigorously. "Now, which ones are you giving me?"

The little girl picked up two dingy plush dolls that had red frilly hair made from yarn and a triangle for a nose. One wore blue overalls and a red and white checkered shirt while the other doll had a flowery dress with a white apron. The two plush dolls also had matching red and white striped socks.

Jenny handed them to the ruler of Hell and said, "I've never liked these. I don't know why but their faces kinda scare me. They were my mom's toys when she was growing up."

Lucifer took them and smiled, "Yes, these will do nicely. Now, take my hand Jenny."

The child took the fallen angel's hand as he opened a portal. They stepped through it and immediately Jenny was awestruck by what she was seeing. People were freely walking around in a small village that was nestled in a vast forest.

Each person looked similar with long flowing hair, pointy ears, and colorful attire. Lucifer produced a wooden staff and jabbed the end on the ground several times, causing magical sparks to crackle with each strike.

The residents of the village turned and looked in the fallen angel's direction, showing little emotions. Lucifer cheerfully marched in their direction with Jenny still clutching his hand. She gasped when several tiny people buzzed around her, their translucent wings fluttering.

"Fairies!" Jenny exclaimed, "Are those fairies?"

"I do believe so, though they could be pixies." Lucifer replied as several villagers approached them.

"Who are you and what are you doing here?" One man spoke.

"Just dropping off a little urchin that's in need of a good home. Anyone willing to take Jenny in?" Lucifer answered.

"Where are her parents?" A woman asked as she pointed at the ruler of Hell. "I can see that she's not your offspring. Where did you snatch her from?"

"Oh please," Lucifer grinned, "like the Fae are above kidnapping children. You've done that for centuries."

The child giggled as the fairies landed on her, examining Jenny closely.

"Why does the ruler of Hell want to hand over a child to us?" The male fae spoke again,

"We have no business working with you, Lucifer."

"Be that as it may, the child wrote me a letter and I'm here to grant her Christmas wish." The fallen angel said. Before the fae could reply, he added, "It's a long story but Jenny wants a friend that will accept her for who she is and will care about her. What better place than this village? Everyone can take turns caring and raising her better than her biological parents. She's been physically, mentally, and emotionally abused by them. If you don't believe me, examine her and the truth will reveal itself."

Gasps escaped from the fairies as one cried out, "Horcus! He speaks the truth! This little one is covered in scars and bruises."

Horcus kneeled down in front of Jenny and asked, "May I see? Just pull your collar down, if you don't mind."

Jenny complied but didn't look at the male fae. Audible gasps escaped from all the onlookers at the purple and green bruises that marred her skin.

"Mirdym, take the child to the healers at once!" Horcus ordered.

As several fae women reached for her, Jenny cried out, "Please, don't hurt me!"

"Jenny, is it?" One woman asked. When the child nodded, she continued to say, "We don't hurt children. We, as a people, feel that children should be cherished and cared for because they are precious to us. We don't have children often because we live a long time so we go out of our way to protect and keep them safe."

"But I'm different," Jenny's lips quivered as she pointed at her groin, "down here."

"Doesn't matter to us," Horcus replied calmly, "You are not defined by what is down there naturally. The Fae can shift our orientation whenever we feel the need to and no one makes a fuss over it. Our fluidity in this is both freeing and empowering. You will discover that as you grow accustomed to us and our ways, Jenny. We want to tend to your wounds and ensure that you are well and not suffering. Will you go with these women to get checked out?"

"Will it hurt?" The child asked.

"Possibly, but pain is to be expected during any form of healing. Rest assured that you won't suffer as you already have at the hands of your parents." Horcus said and then he looked up at Lucifer with anger in his eyes and asked, "Are they still alive?"

"For the moment," the fallen angel answered as he shook the two plush dolls with a devilish grin, "I plan on dealing with them shortly. It might not be the sort of punishment that your goddess of Justice would hand out, but it will be a fitting punishment."

Horcus nodded curtly as the women escorted Jenny away and he said, "Good. If not, I'd go there and end them myself."

Lucifer turned around and opened a portal and stepped through it. As he entered the apartment, the sound of someone banging on the front door met his ears as a muffled voice shouted, "Police! Open the door!"

The ruler of Hell saw that the parents were on their knees, their faces were battered and bruised. Paroxysm sat in a chair behind them with her eyes pulsating as a tendril of energy traveled from her and into the parent's backs, holding them in place.

Lucifer walked over and sat the dolls in front of them and said coldly, "It's time to get your punishment started. Paroxysm, will you connect to the dolls?"

"As you command, sire," the she-devil replied. The same tendrils painfully pierced through their stomachs and into the plush dolls.

He placed his hands on the couple's heads and spoke, "You *will* die by my hand but your suffering is just beginning. Your souls shall be placed into these dolls before you. There, you will reside until these cheap vessels fall apart. When that occurs, you'll be coming straight to Hell for the next phase of your punishment. Paroxysm will handle you as she sees fit. Your souls have been personally earmarked by me so forget any notions of Heaven. You are both *mine.*"

Lucifer spoke in Enochian, his eyes glowing brightly white, as Jenny's parents convulsed in place. The banging on the front door grew louder as an officer shouted, "Police! We're coming in!"

The dolls shimmered slightly as the souls entered them. Lucifer looked directly at his minion and ordered, "Release them."

The tendrils recoiled back into the she-devil. The corpses dropped hard on the floor, breaking both their noses. Blood seeped from the wounds as the front door swung open. Several police officers stepped inside with their weapons drawn.

The fallen angel had the next envelope in hand as he created a portal when one of the officers ordered, "Get down! Get down on the floor now!"

"I'm sorry to disappoint you but we have a tight schedule to keep. Come along, Paroxysm." Lucifer said, barely acknowledging the officers as he put the envelope away.

"You're not going anywhere! Get down on the floor now!" A second officer barked.

Paroxysm eyed the humans and seductively purred, "Can I stay behind? I do love a good man in an authoritative uniform, especially when I eviscerate them."

"Not now. Maybe later. Let these nice mortals clean up our mess," Lucifer replied as he walked towards the portal.

"Tis the season of giving, boys. Enjoy our gift to you, from Hell." Paroxysm hissed at police, baring her razor-sharp teeth as she followed behind the ruler of Hell. The officers rushed over as the duo vanished before their disbelieving eyes.

"Jack? Please tell me you saw that? You saw that right?" One officer asked as he walked over to where the duo from Hell disappeared.

"I did, Steve," Jack replied as he stared at his partner as Steve waved his hand around, trying to figure out where they went. Jack added as he scratched his head, "But I'm not looking forward to filling out the report on this murder."

Chapter Eleven

Speaking In Tongues

Lucifer and the she-devil stepped out of the portal and were greeted by humid but slightly chilly weather, a far cry from most of their wintery stops so far.

The fallen angel sniffed the muggy air and said with a cheerful smile, "Ah, the sweet aroma of raging hormones and subtle taste of death. We're definitely in Florida."

"Too bad that it's not spring break," Paroxysm replied as she looked out at the swaying palm trees off in the distance, knowing that a beach was nearby, "I'd have a lot of fun sinking my claws and teeth in the party goers."

"Keep up the good work tonight and I'll allow you to come back here for some well-deserved frivolity." Lucifer said as he touched her on the shoulder. "For now, let's finish up and get back to Hell."

Paroxysm smiled brightly at the ruler of Hell as she squealed with delight, "I can't wait to use a few of those muscle men as a surfboard. So, what gift are you handing out here?"

Lucifer pulled out the envelope and opened it up as he kept walking, keeping his eyes focused on a small townhouse. He took out the letter and leveled it to his eyes. As he read, the ruler of Hell paused mid-stride.

"What is it, sire?" Paroxysm asked hesitantly.

"Something that needs to be accomplished but first, I'll need to see if what the little urchin's saying is true or not." Lucifer said, his visage unreadable.

The neighborhood houses all had Christmas decorations on them and in the yards. If it weren't for the holiday decor, one wouldn't even know that it was Christmas time at all. There were shiny new vehicles aligning either side of the street with a few older models sitting on the driveways.

Even the palm trees had multicolored lights strung around them, adding to the festive time of the year. Dogs barked as the duo from Hell strolled down the sidewalk but a quick, menacing glance from the she-devil, each dog whimpered as they cowered in fear.

Paroxysm grinned at her master but then she froze. Lucifer paused when he noticed that she wasn't next to him.

"What is it?" Lucifer asked with confusion.

"Listen, sire. Do you hear it?"

The fallen angel listened intently with his eyes closed. He tuned out all of the normal background noises and hear what he believed Paroxysm picked up.

"A muttering child?" The ruler of Hell asked.

"Yes," the she-devil answered as she pointed at a yellow house that had ceramic roof tiles and a stucco exterior. "I'm feeling drawn to his tortured crying like a siren's song. May I go to him while you make your delivery?"

Lucifer focused on the child and then at the letter before responding, "No. We'll both be seeing him. If I'm correct, it's little Daniel

Perry. The one that sent me the Christmas wish. Now, I'm intrigued to hear more. Lead the way, Paroxysm but try not to frighten him."

Paroxysm straightened out her jacket and said, "I only frighten those that deserve it. From what I can feel, this Daniel Perry is beyond what I would willingly cause a person, especially an innocent child."

"Try your best." Lucifer replied as they neared the house. As they stepped on the driveway, the duo from Hell paused at the barely audible sound of sniffling. The fallen angel walked past a beat-up Ford minivan and approached a locked wooden gate that led into the backyard.

Lucifer snatched the padlock in his hand and ripped it off the latch with ease. He let it drop on the gravel path with a clanking thud as he pushed open the gate. Paroxysm strolled in behind him and was drawn to a large, mahogany-stained, wooden patio deck that had hedges and several lamp posts lining it.

She got down on her knees and saw a young boy, no more than six, sitting with his back against a support beam. Daniel had his head buried against his knees as he rocked back and forth, his arms around his little gangly legs.

"Daniel," Paroxysm called out, trying to get his attention. The boy jumped, causing him to bang his head on the wooden patio planks above him. The she-devil cringed as Daniel crying loudly.

"Paroxysm," Lucifer chided, "I thought I told you specifically *not* to scare the boy."

"It's not my fault, sire," the she-devil pleaded as he scowled at her. "How was I to know that he's got a bad case of PTSD?"

The fallen angel's menacing white eyes stared intently at his minion before he looked away. Daniel was lying flat on the ground, still holding his head crying. Lucifer took a calm breath as he plastered a genuine smile of merriment as he boldly announced, "Ho, ho, ho! Where's Daniel Perry at? Santa got a letter from him. Do you know where he's at, little boy under the patio?"

Daniel quietened down. He rolled over on his side, sniffling as he answered with a shaky voice, "Santa? Is that you?"

"Depends," Lucifer smirked as he pulled out the envelope. "I'm here to grant the Christmas wish that little Daniel Perry asked for."

The boy's teary eyes widened with excitement as he proclaimed, "That's my letter! I'm Daniel! I'm Daniel!"

"Come on out from there before you give yourself another boo-boo," Lucifer coaxed as he reached out his hand.

As Daniel crawled over, loud banging and muffled shouting came from within the house. He paused and held his dirty palms over his ears. The fallen angel glanced at Paroxysm and she said, "I'll silence them, sire."

As she jumped up and onto the patio, Lucifer said, "They'll need to be alive for this Christmas wish."

"I shall endeavor to restrain my primal urges, sire." Paroxysm dramatically bowed before opening the sliding glass door. Lucifer rolled his eyes as Daniel took his hand and came out.

The fallen angel escorted the boy out of the backyard towards the sidewalk. They found a bench seat for a bus stop and sat down together.

Lucifer looked at Daniel and asked, "You are Daniel Perry, correct?"

He nodded, "Yes. Are you truly Santa Claus?"

"No, I'm not." The fallen angel replied. As the boy lowered his head, Lucifer added, "I'm here because you wrote me this letter. I've read what you want and, quite frankly, it's good that you're dealing with me instead of Santa. He's a magical being of the Fae, but he can't do what it is that you truly desire so I'm filling in for him."

"Santa really does exist?" Daniel cried out in excitement.

"Yes. But this year, I'm having to take care of a few deliveries that the jolly fat man can't do because the wishes were sent to me. That said," the ruler of Hell pulled out the letter and read it aloud, "you want your parents to be nice to each other and to you?"

"Yes. They are constantly yelling at each other and hitting and breaking things." Daniel slouched his shoulders as he looked at the cracked pavement at his feet. "I don't like it. I'm scared. I don't want to get hit again."

“Hmm,” the ruler of Hell muttered to himself, mulling over how to fix this situation short of killing Daniel’s parents. They turned to look back at the house as the screaming grew to a crescendo before all went silent. Lucifer glanced down at Daniel and said with a smile, “I believe that Paroxysm has settled the fighting down significantly. Let’s head inside and see if we can make your greatest wish come true.”

Daniel stood up reluctantly, looking down at his feet, not daring to look up at his home. Lucifer placed his hand on the little boy’s heavy shoulder and ushered him forward. As they walked up the driveway, the ruler of Hell could feel Daniel tensing up with each step.

“Don’t fret, dear boy.” Lucifer stated as they stepped up on the concrete porch, “All that I need for you to do when we go inside is to be brave. I won’t allow them to harm you.”

Despite hearing this, Daniel’s anxiety didn’t wane. Lucifer grabbed the doorknob and yanked open the front door. The house had garland and Christmas lights hanging from the trim along the walls, a few family portraits, along with holes the size of a man’s fist, made up the rest of open spaces. The fragrance of potpourri, cheap alcohol, and stale cigarette smoke filled the air.

Splinters of glass on the floor glinted in the light from several broken tumblers that had been thrown against the wall. Several wooden chairs were knocked over on the floor by a long mahogany table where the adults were glaring at Paroxysm and brandishing butcher knives.

"I don't know who the fuck you are or what the hell you're doing in our house, bitch, but if you come any closer, I *will* kill you!" An angry man shouted at the she-devil.

"Please," Paroxysm cackled as she flashed her razor-sharp teeth, causing Daniel's parents to cower. "You'll be dead before you can make a move on me with your pathetic culinary tools. My master is here to do a job, whether either of you like it or not."

"Quite right, Paroxysm." Lucifer announced as he and Daniel moved forward. He looked at the adults with both contempt and boredom, "I'm only here for little Daniel, not you two hairless apes."

"Daniel," his mother pleaded with the boy. "Get over here! You don't know these *freaks*!"

Daniel moved to hide behind Lucifer, visibly shaking. The ruler of Hell stepped slightly in front of the boy protectively as he said, "I believe that Daniel finds more comfort with the Devil than he would with either of you."

"You're insane!" The man cried out, "Are you implying that you *are* the Devil himself? You don't look anything like that beast. Just an ordinary man that's sick in the head."

"Ah, and pray tell what does the Devil look like?" Lucifer asked, feeling amused.

"He's a hideous creature with horns on his head, red skin, cloven feet and wooly legs like a goat." The mother replied as she spat on the floor.

"He also has a pitch fork, a red cape, and long tail with a spike on the end of it. Everyone, including imbeciles, knows this, which is why we know that you are just pretending to be the Devil, you crazy fuck!" The father added.

"See, sire?" The she-devil quipped, "You're too formally dressed for these mortals. Guess that you should've worn your favorite Halloween costume."

Lucifer rolled his eyes and said, "Let me guess: you learned all this from church?"

"We learned everything from the Bible and from our religious leaders over the years. We go to church every Wednesday and Sunday like the good people that we are. This is a God-fearing house and we do as his good word says, asshole!" The father retorted passionately.

The ruler of Hell chuckled, shaking his head, "You humans are so diluted. The only one in this house that's actually fearful is your child. Besides, going to church doesn't make either of you good people any more than standing in a garage makes you a Lamborghini."

The father rushed forward past the she-devil and lunged at Lucifer, stabbing him multiple times in the chest and the stomach. The father back away, leaving the butcher knife buried in the ruler of Hell's chest.

The man looked bewildered and shocked as Lucifer glared at him flatly as he pulled out the knife slowly and stated, "If you're quite finished breaking one of my Father's ten commandments, I have a gift to grant Daniel. Hold them in place, Paroxysm."

"With pleasure, sire." The she-devil said as she grabbed both of the adults and pinned them roughly against the wall.

The couple grunted in pain as they attempted to recite the Lord's prayer out loud. Paroxysm got in their faces and threatened them coldly, "Shut up right now, you two mouth breathers or I *will* peel your tongues out and forcefully make you eat them."

The father sneered arrogantly, "You will be cast back into Hell. Our Lord will – OOMPH!"

The she-devil rammed her knee into the man's groin and said, "It won't have that effect on either of us so zip it! Hypocrisy gives me a headache and, right now, I'm getting a migraine in this house."

"Leave their tongues intact but feel free to silence them in other ways." Lucifer ordered.

Paroxysm grumbled as the fallen angel turned and kneeled down in front of Daniel. He pulled the envelope out of his pocket and removed the letter and read it.

He eyed the boy and asked, "So, your Christmas wish is for your parents to never fight or hurt each other ever again. Tell me Daniel, have they ever hurt you?"

"Sometimes." Daniel replied with a little shrug, not looking directly at Lucifer. "I'm tired of seeing them crying and screaming. I want to have a happy family, like my other friends have, sir."

"I see." The fallen angel stood up and walked over to Daniel's parents. He reached out and nicked them each on the cheek, drawing blood. He ran a finger over the cuts and slowly walked backwards towards the boy, his eyes glowing white. He never took his steely gaze off the adults as he ordered, "Step forward, Daniel, and tell them what you want from this night forward."

"Leave our son out of this evil! The mother cried out. "Just leave us all alone, you miserable fucks!"

Daniel looked up at Lucifer, who nodded to encourage him to speak, "I want us to be happy! I want no more fighting! No more hitting, swearing, or breaking things! Why can't we be happy?"

The fallen angel rose up in the air, his tendril wings glowed ethereally as he announced, "With this blood magic, your wish shall be granted, Daniel."

The parents clutched their heads, crying out in excruciating pain. Paroxysm maliciously smiled as she kept them upright and pinned to the wall. The entire house shook like it was in the epicenter of an earthquake. The boy worried about his parents but didn't dare go over to them. He wrapped his little arms around Lucifer's right leg as he descended back to the floor.

The ruler of Hell's eyes pulsated as he spoke, "Release them, Paroxysm. Let them step forward and speak."

The she-devil shrugged her shoulders as she did as she was told. The adults clutched each other, fearing what Lucifer would do next as they meekly moved towards the fallen angel.

"Are you going to say something or has the hellcat devoured your tongues?" Lucifer mocked with a sneer.

"What did you do to us, you coupon banana?" The father attempted to yell but his voice came out soft and smooth. Confusion crossed his visage as he spoke again, "Daisy butterfly! Salmon smelly colon puffs!"

Daniel couldn't control his giggle fit as his mother spoke, her voice sounding exactly like her husband, "Kitty poke lily pads! I'm a goof of a booger!"

"Here's how this works," Lucifer stated as he stood before the parents. "As long as you try to fight or think negative thoughts, you *both* will speak in this manner. The only way to prevent this is to love each other and Daniel. If you try to hit one another or throw things around like spoiled brats having a tantrum, you will be compelled to give hugs and shower each other in affection."

"Harry Potter lambasted a crawdad's uncle for thirty ponies!" The father said as his body trembled.

Daniel laughed even more as Lucifer spoke once again, "That shaking will only get worse as you fight the spell. Trust me when I say that pain won't be far behind. I suggest you two grow up and act like loving parents for once in your pathetic lives."

The mother dropped to the floor with her arms stretched out, beckoning Daniel as tears streamed down her face, "Daniel, I want to hug you! Come to mommy!"

As the boy ran over to his mother, Lucifer announced, "See? It's not that complicated, is it? Just know that this applies to others outside of your home. I'm sure that you don't want the general public to hear your little word salad."

"How long will this last?" Daniel asked as he nuzzled against his mother.

"For the rest of their lives." The fallen angel answered as his gaze fell on the father.

"Broccoli doughnuts and cheese nuts!" The father bit out, his shaking intensified, "Balloon gardens blossom horse feathers!"

"Such language!" Lucifer scoffed as Daniel kept on laughing. He grabbed the father roughly by his jaw and said coldly, "Keep it up and you'll wish that you were never born."

"Will it kill him?" The mother asked, concern etched on her face.

"No, it won't. Your husband is doing this all to himself, at this point. He's the only one that can stop the pain. Neither of you can end your life so this is a choice that needs to be made for the spell to stop. That's the only escape from his current plight. Those are the rules. Am I clear on this?"

As the mother nodded, Paroxysm added as she tapped a claw on her chin thoughtfully while looking around at the house, "It might be that he's an idiot and can't remember. Perhaps it would help to have lists posted everywhere so that a man as thick-headed as him can figure it out, eventually."

"Sounds like a brilliant idea, Paroxysm." Lucifer responded as he looked over at Daniel and added, "Do you think that you can help your more affectionate mother with this little project to help out your dear old dad?"

Daniel's eyes brightened as he ran out of the room. The ruler of Hell patiently waited for the boy to return as the mother stood up. She hung her head meekly and said, "I want to thank you. Thank you for saving our family. I don't know what I can do to repay this kindness."

"Do right by Daniel from here on out and that will suffice. If either of you don't, the next time I see you won't be pleasant. Paroxysm will see to it. In *Hell*." The fallen angel replied.

"I don't understand," Daniel's mother replied, looking confused. "Why are you doing this? Why are you being so *nice*? I could've sworn that you were–"

"Evil incarnate?" Lucifer interrupted. She nodded as he continued to explain, "I'm a necessary evil for my Father but my true purpose in Hell is to punish those that deserve it. Sure, I've been known to tempt humans into doing a few bad things, but that was to show that you people are fully capable of performing whatever dark desires that's already festering in your brains. Humans are not perfect, which is why it's amusing to test your kind. I've gotten blamed for many terrible deeds throughout the centuries because it's easy to blame someone else rather than take responsibility for your choices. Your actions."

"I see. I'm sorry that I misjudged you." The mother said.

"Buffalo crying mangos!" The father cried out as he curled up in a fetal position, clutching his abdomen. "Green tonsils have fluffy marshmallow fleas!"

Daniel rushed back in the living room, carrying a stack of construction paper and a box of markers. He beamed a bright smile as he said, "Come on, mommy! Let's make some signs like that nice scary lady said to do!"

Paroxysm blushed ever so slightly as she warmly smiled at the boy. She turned, heading straight for the front door, leaving the ruler of Hell with the family.

Lucifer was about to go, but paused. He looked down at Daniel and asked, "Is this sufficient? Did I grant your Christmas wish?"

Daniel looked up from the sign he was working on. He observed his mother laying down construction paper, seemingly content with the project while his father was whimpering and unable to do anything else and said, "I think so, sir. We'll get daddy better."

"I'm sure that he will. Hopefully, his stubbornness shall subside, but until then, have a laugh or two at what he says. I've fulfilled our deal and now we must go. Take care, Daniel."

The boy jumped to his feet and ran over to Lucifer. He wrapped his little arms around the fallen angel's waist and then made a beeline to the she-devil. Paroxysm chuckled as she lifted Daniel up and held onto him like he was a precious item to cherish.

"Thank you, nice scary lady! I love you!" Daniel said with a heart melting smile.

Lucifer smirked as he stood next to the confused, blushing she-devil. She sat him back down on the floor and fled hastily out the front door with the ruler of Hell trailing behind her. Lucifer closed the door and could see Paroxysm leaning against a metal lamp post across the street.

He strolled up to her and asked, "Are you well? Do you need a moment or someone to flay?"

The she-devil wiped the tears from her face and said, "I'm okay, sire. That was…unexpected, to say the least."

"I can see that. Do you feel that you can finish the task at hand or do you –"

"I'm fine, sire!" Paroxysm gruffly said, cutting off the ruler of Hell. "How many more children are there to go now?"

Lucifer reached into his leather jacket pocket and pulled out the remaining envelopes and said, "Three more to go and then we can call it a night."

Paroxysm nodded curtly and said, "I can do this, sire. I won't fail you."

Lucifer put his hand on her shoulder and said sympathetically, "I never doubted your abilities for this and I still don't. This human holiday is strange but in a good way. It definitely has had an effect on both of us tonight."

"Let's finish the job and then I'll decompress in the best way possible." The she-devil replied as she moved away from the lamp post.

As Lucifer created a portal to take them to the next child on the list, he asked, "And what way would that be?"

"Grant you the pelt of Rabbit once we have the trickster. Think of it as my Christmas gift from me to you, sire."

Lucifer nodded as he placed his hand on the small of her back and they both stepped into the portal.

Chapter Twelve

Did Someone Order A Bride?

The duo from Hell stepped out of the portal and on a frozen sidewalk. Paroxysm lost her footing and fell flat on her ass. She roared as she slammed her fists on the ice. Lucifer stood by silently with his hands behind his back.

"I'm so fucking sick of this wintery weather up here!" The she-devil snarled as she attempted to stand up but ended up back on her ass with a grunt of frustration.

"Do you need a hand getting up?" The fallen angel asked hesitantly as he tried to hide his amusement.

"I'm fine!" Paroxysm snapped as rolled over onto her belly and crawled unsteadily over to a patch of grass where Lucifer stood. She grunted as the frozen blades of grass crunched under her weight.

The she-devil huffed as she hung her head and said, "My apologies, sire. I didn't mean to disrespect you like that with my attitude. Punish me as you see fit."

"Oh, Paroxysm." The ruler of Hell spoke as he put a hand on her head. "You don't need to fear me. You're helping me with this little project tonight. A little slip is to be expected."

Paroxysm grumbled as she stood up while Lucifer chuckled. She brushed the loose bits of ice off of her garments and asked, "Can we finish this? I'm missing the heat and the anguish screaming from home. Where are we now?"

"Interesting enough, not in the United States. We're in a quaint little town in Russia." The fallen angel said.

Lucifer pulled out the envelope and looked at it and saw that it had been mailed from Russia. He shrugged his shoulders as he scanned the area. Each of the houses in the neighborhood had Christmas lights adorning the trim of the roofs and in the windows. Inflatable and wood carved decorations covered several lawns while others had multicolored light fixtures sticking out of the ground.

All the houses appeared cheerful and in the Christmas spirit, save one. The house was completely dark with no decorations or anything that represented the festive holiday. The grass on the frozen lawn was thick and needed to be mowed. There was a beat up, multicolored pickup truck parked by the side of the house where part of the gutter was precariously dangling off the eaves.

"So, what does this kid want? A pony? A bazooka?" Paroxysm grumbled as her foul mood took hold.

Lucifer pulled out the letter and read it. He paused and cocked his head to the side, "This one will be interesting, to say the least."

"Oh, how vague of you, sire."

The ruler of Hell turned and said with a smile, "I can understand that you're done with all this festive fun so, if you can indulge me, go back to Hell for me. I need you to go fetch me one of my minions that can fulfill this wish. Will you do it for me, please?"

He handed the letter over to the she-devil as her eyes lit up with delight. She read over the request and said, "I believe that I know the perfect match. I won't let you down, sire!"

The fallen angel took the letter back and said, "Take some time and recharge down there while I go speak to little Cindy about this one."

Paroxysm exaggerated a curtsey and said, "Thy will shall be done, oh gracious one!"

Lucifer rolled his eyes as he shook his head as the she-devil disappeared back into the depths of Hell. He walked on the lawn towards the front door, the icy grass crunching with each step. The fallen angel stepped up on the wooden porch, the rotting planks creaked under his weight but didn't splinter much.

The address on the house caused Lucifer to laugh to himself, "666. It's like they were expecting me all along."

Lucifer put his hand on the doorknob and magically unlocked the deadbolt and the lock in the nob itself. The ruler of Hell opened the door and stepped inside quietly. The interior of the house was just as dreary as the outside. The floors were carpeted and had numerous stains and dark spots from heavy foot traffic.

On the mantle of the fireplace were several family pictures, each one had Cindy and her parents happily smiling in them. The ceiling was in need of repairs as brown water spots covered it in various places.

Toys and discarded food wrappers laid strewn on the scuffed-up table along with several plates that had partially eaten food on them. Lucifer heard a slight shuffling of tiny feet making their way towards him. He looked down and saw a small girl with only a long nightshirt and bunny slippers walking in the kitchen as she tried to rub the sleep from her eyes.

The ruler of Hell noticed that her eyes were also puffy with dark circles under them. The child picked up a blue cup and took a couple of sips from it. She turned and saw Lucifer sitting down at the kitchen table, smiling as he asked, "Hello, little one. Are you Cindy?"

The girl nodded as she answered with a tired voice, "I'm not ahspose to talk to strangers."

"Well, that's good to hear. I'm not a stranger!" Lucifer spoke as he pulled out the envelope and slid it to her, "Is this your Christmas letter that you wrote?"

Cindy's eyes widened, "Yes! Are you Santa? You don't much look like him."

"Very astute observation, Cindy. I got your letter and I'm here to grant your Christmas wish! Isn't that delightful?"

"But, if you're not Santa, then who are you?" The girl inquired as she set the envelope down.

"My name is Lucifer. Since you misspelled the jolly man's name, I got your request instead. Tonight, I've been granting those wishes as Santa takes care of the other trivial ones."

Lucifer picked up the envelope and pulled out the letter. He read over it, glancing up at the child several times before asking, "Am I reading this correctly?"

"I dunno, sir. My spelling is not so good." Cindy replied as she rubbed her arm unconsciously.

"You say that your Papa is so sad all the time? You want him to be happy again?"

The child looked at Lucifer directly in his eyes and explained, "Yes! Papa has been sad ever since Mama went to Heaven two years ago. Can you make Papa happy?"

"Perhaps," the fallen angel tapped a finger on his chin. "It will all hinge on your Papa. I can help him but he's the only one that can get himself out of his sadness."

"Oh." Cindy replied, feeling a little dejected. "I didn't know that."

The fallen angel stood up and walked over to the little girl. He patted her on the head and reassured Cindy, "How could you know? Are you what? Six?"

"I will be next month, sir!" Cindy clapped loudly as she jumped for joy.

"Really?" Lucifer mischievously eyed the little girl and asked, "And what would you like for your birthday?"

Cindy's eyes widened with excitement, "Are you going to come back for my birthday with a toy too?"

"No, I plan on giving you one tonight!" The fallen angel proclaimed with a snap of his finger. "Tell me what *you* want?"

Cindy crossed her little arms across her chest, trying to think of something. She winced slightly, which caught Lucifer's attention.

"Little Cindy, are you hurt?" The ruler of Hell inquired.

She shrugged her shoulders and said, "I'm okay. I gotta be strong so Papa won't worry so much."

The fallen angel scoffed, "Cindy, that's all well and noble of you but you don't need to be. You should be a child first and be happy. Now tell me, who it is that's been hurting you, little one."

"A bunch of older kids like to push me down to the ground and hit me and...do weird things."

Lucifer narrowed his eyes ever so slightly, "What do you mean by *weird things*?"

"I don't know how to ascribe it, sir." Cindy replied as she fidgeted with her nightshirt.

The ruler of Hell kneeled down in front of the little girl and asked as he placed his index finger on his forehead, "Cindy, may I put my finger here on your forehead like this?" When she nodded sadly, Lucifer added, "I won't hurt you but this may feel funny on your head. I'm going to look at your memories and see *exactly* what those older kids have been doing to you. Are you ready?"

"Yes, I am. No tell Papa. I don't want Papa worried about me." Cindy requested.

"Fret not," the fallen angel assured her as he put his finger up to his lips, "It will be our little secret."

Lucifer put his index finger on Cindy's forehead and probed her mind. He concentrated on her most recent memories and was disturbed by what he found.

Cindy giggled, "That tickles!"

"I'm glad one of us finds this amusing." The fallen angel replied flatly.

Lucifer stood back up and used his senses to find Cindy's tormentors. It didn't take long but it also didn't surprise him that all the older kids lived on the same street. A devilish smile slowly creeped across Lucifer's visage as an idea formed.

"Excuse me for a moment, Cindy." Lucifer said as he walked towards the front door, "I have to meet with someone outside that I don't want you to see. She might be scary looking but she will help keep those ruffians off you until they learn their lesson."

"What lady?" Cindy asked.

"If you are familiar with your regional folklore, then you'll know the name of a nocnitsa," the ruler of Hell responded.

The little girl gasped. She ran into her bedroom for a moment and rushed back into the kitchen, clutching a small stone with a hole bore in it.

Lucifer nodded, "I'm impressed, but don't fret. Krisky won't be coming in here to harm you, child. Now, be a good little girl and wake up your Papa."

She nodded but kept her little hands tightly on the stone as she walked towards her father's bedroom down the hall. Lucifer opened the front door and, within fifteen seconds of stepping outside, was greeted by the nocnitsa.

The nocnitsa swayed back and forth in her ethereal form, all shadow and no physical form with two distinct glowing red eyes. The air around here had the aroma of moss and dirt.

As Lucifer approached her, the nocnitsa spoke which came out as a screech with each syllable uttered, "You summoned for me, *Lightbringer*?"

"Indeed, I have, Krisky." The ruler of Hell replied. "My, you look a little famished. Are you not feeding enough, my dear?"

Krisky sighed, "This time of year is difficult to feed because of all the merrymaking and happiness. It's hard to find suitable sombering meals."

"You're in luck, then. I have the perfect gifts for you on the festive holiday. Ones that you won't be able to resist," Lucifer said as he walked over to her.

"Yes," the nocnitsa said as she looked at the house behind him, moving towards it, "the occupants of this domicile will strengthen me for a long time."

Lucifer's eyes glowed brightly, stopping the nocnitsa, "This house is off limits and not to be fed on by you or any of your ilk, *Night Hag*!"

"But I don't understand." The nocnitsa responded, feeling confused, "If you want me to feed, then why bring me to a house that's filled with sorrow and depression and order me away from it?"

"Because you have other meals waiting for you on this long stretch of road that needs your *special* attention. Six, to be precise. They're causing the little girl here pain and sexual inappropriateness that she doesn't deserve. I made a promise to stop her torment and that's where you come in." The fallen angel held out his hand and added, "These are your meals. I'm sure that before spring, you'll be so engorged by these individuals that you'll be as fat as a politician. What do you say, Krisky?"

The nocnitsa cackled, which sounded like a person playing a violin with the blades of a garbage disposal, "A generous gift, especially from one such as yourself, Lucifer. Are you sure that I can't taste this house?"

Lucifer grabbed the nocnitsa as he unfurled his tendril wings, his eyes blazing white as he vehemently threatened, "Do it and I'll see to it that you starve and never receive any further sustenance. You will only be able to find them but be incapable of feeding! This house is under *my* protection! If you or any of your other nocnitsas attempt to feed here, I *will* make good on my threat and bring it down on *all* of you! Do you comprehend what I'm saying, Krisky?"

The nocnitsa's shadowy form squirmed and wavered under the power of the ruler of Hell. She bit out apologetically, "My lord, I beseech you! No more, please! It will be done! You have my word!"

Lucifer pulled the nocnitsa mere inches from his face and coldly whispered, "Spread the word, Krisky. I don't appreciate having my deals meddled with! The six meals need to know that they aren't allowed to harm the little one in here. Get creative and do my bidding, *now*!"

The nocnitsa coughed as Lucifer pushed it away. Paroxysm appeared next to the fallen angel and said, "Did I miss you playing with one of the local entities?"

"Just making a deal with Krisky to go after the boys hurting and molesting little Cindy." Lucifer said. He looked over at the new person next to the she-devil and asked, "Nice choice, Paroxysm. Come along and let's all go inside and get to know the family."

The ruler of Hell marched back towards the small house and opened the front door. He walked in and found Cindy talking to her father as he was rubbing the sleep from his droopy eyes.

"I'm not fibbing, Papa!" The little girl exclaimed, "Lucifer wanted me to wake you up so he can grant my Christmas wish."

"My daughter," the father spoke, his Russian accent made him sound even more tired. "you were probably just dreaming. How's about I make us some tea and we both go back to bed? It's too early for gifts."

"But, Papa–"

"No!" The man cut off his daughter as he stood up from the kitchen chair, not even noticing the denizens of Hell walking towards them, "We can discuss all of this nonsense later."

"I'm on a tight schedule so you'll have to wait on the tea, sir." Lucifer spoke.

The father froze mid step. He turned his head and saw the fallen angel standing at the threshold of the kitchen, smiling at him. He could see two other figures behind Lucifer but they were obscured by the darkness of the living room.

The fallen angel kneeled down by Cindy and said as he put his hand on her little shoulder, "I've taken care of your *birthday wish*. You can rest well now that it has been taken care of. And now, it's time to fulfill your Christmas wish."

"Who are you and what are you doing in *my* house?" The father asked as he shuffled over to Cindy protectively.

Lucifer stood and said, "I'm sure that your daughter already told you who I am but, just in case you have doubts," his eyes glowed brightly white, "I'm Lucifer and I'm here to grant Cindy's Christmas wish."

The father's eyes widened while his daughter squealed as she said, "See, Papa? I told you that Lucifer is here for us!"

"What is your name, sir?" The ruler of Hell asked.

"Chr–Christoph." He stammered as his body shook with fear, "Christoph Molvalet."

Lucifer pulled out the envelope and read Cindy's letter out loud, "Right. This letter to me says: Dear Satan, I know that you are busy this year. What I want the mostest is for my Papa to be happy! Mama went to Heaven and he's been sad since. Can you help Papa? Love, Cindy Molvalet."

Christoph's mouth gaped open as he looked down at Cindy and asked, "You asked the Devil himself to make me happy? Why would you do such a thing, child?"

"I thought only of you, Papa." Cindy replied, feeling uncomfortable under her father's gaze. "It was ahspose to go to Santa but I didn't spell it good. Don't be mad, Papa!"

He kneeled down beside her and vehemently answered, "I'm not mad at you, daughter! I'm just shocked by all of this. I never thought that you would do this, ask for my happiness."

Lucifer put his hand on Christoph's shoulder and said, "If it's all the same to you, I need to make a few more deliveries so do stand up and get ready for your Christmas gift that Cindy asked for."

Christoph stood up and warily asked, "Do you require my soul or hers for this *gift*?"

Lucifer scoffed as he replied indignantly, "I swear, does *everyone* on Earth believe this nonsense? I don't steal souls to bring to Hell. Humanity has been doing a bang-up job all on their own since my Father created you! I do enjoy tempting humans but that's it. Humans are an evil sickness like no other race! Is it truly a wonder why I don't have to lift a finger to claim the wicked that rightfully deserve to be punished?"

Lucifer felt a tap on his shoulder that caught his attention. He glanced over and saw the she-devil pointing at her wrist and say, "Time's ticking, sire."

"Right," the fallen angel nodded curtly, "now, without further delay, I present to you Lylia!"

Lucifer stepped out of the way so that Christoph could see her. His eyes were transfixed on the strange woman as she approached him. Christoph felt his heart racing and his mouth going dry with each step that Lylia took towards him.

Lylia got two feet from Cindy's father and slowly turned around, giving him a view of her entire body. She wore only a one-piece black suit that accentuated her many curves and calf-high boots to match. Her bouncy curly hair was a deep shade of crimson and her eyes were as sparkly as two shimmering emeralds. Lylia barely let her tongue graze out of her mouth, wetting her ruby red lips.

"Does my form please the man of this domicile?" Lylia asked, her voice came out as smooth as silk.

"What? What are you? An angel?" Christoph asked as he reached out and took her hand. He tentatively pressed his lips against her skin but never took his eyes off hers.

As Lylia giggled, Lucifer had to suppress a laugh as he answered, "I'm the only angel in this house. Lylia is actually a succubus. She's been given strict instructions to not only please you, but ensure that you are happy for the rest of your long life."

"Wait, isn't a succubus supposed to–"

"Not in front of the child, Christoph!" Lucifer cut the man off, not wanting to scare Cindy.

Paroxysm moved towards the child and asked, "This part is for the adults. Come along and show me your room, Cindy."

As the she-devil walked out of the kitchen with Cindy, Lucifer said as soon as the child's door closed shut, "A succubus is supposed to slowly devour their victims energetically as they place them under their sexual spells. Lylia has the task to not do this to you. She will fuck you like no mortal has ever been fucked before. That said, Lylia does require *sustenance* so she will have to feed on others so that she can survive."

"So, she will kill others but not me?" Christoph asked, still unable to tear his gaze from Lylia. "Will she try to feed on Cindy?"

"No!" Lylia spoke as she stepped up mere inches from Christoph. "I'm here to make sure that you are happy. How can you be happy if I killed her? Your household is under Lucifer's protection and I will fiercely protect both of you if anyone tries to hurt either of you. This is my unbreakable oath to you and Lucifer. Do you accept these conditions, *darling*?"

"I do, Lylia!" Christoph quickly spoke, not wanting to disappoint this woman before him.

"Do you have any conditions for her, Christoph?" The fallen angel asked.

"No, I don't but I have to ask: do you want to be with me?"

The succubus purred as her emerald eyes pulsated, "I do, my *darling*!"

Lucifer clapped his hands together loudly, "Splendid! Kiss your new *bride* and enjoy all the happy fornications to come. It's how she wanted to seal the oath."

Lylia let Christoph press his lips against hers before firmly kissing him back.

Paroxysm and Cindy came back into the kitchen to witness the kiss and the child asked, "Will that lady make Papa's sadness go away?"

"I'm positive that Lylia can melt all of your father's woes away." The she-devil said as she walked over to the fallen angel.

As the new couple breathlessly parted from each other, Cindy could see more life in her father's face that she hadn't seen in a long time. Christoph looked at Lucifer and gushed, "Thank you, Lucifer!"

"All the credit goes to Cindy but, you're welcome. Come along, Paroxysm."

Lucifer pulled out the next envelope and created a portal. Cindy rushed over and hugged the fallen angel around his waist and shouted, "Thank you, Lucifer! You make Papa happy, I can see!"

"My pleasure, little urchin." Lucifer said. He saw her father and the succubus walking towards his bedroom and he added, "And pretty soon, your Papa will be having his own pleasure too. Off to bed, Cindy."

The child let go of Lucifer reluctantly and watched both him and Paroxysm step through his portal and disappear.

Chapter Thirteen

Oh, Death

The duo from Hell stepped out on a long narrow strip of road as the dark clouds above them let loose a torrent of rain. Lucifer looked around and commented to the she-devil, "Here we are. In Portland, Oregon."

"How can you be sure of that? We could be in Seattle for all we know." Paroxysm replied as she got drenched.

"Because I'm like my Father! All-knowing!" The fallen angel boasted.

"Really, sire?" Paroxysm grumbled, not exactly buying it. "And you've been granted the gift of foresight?"

"I have!" Lucifer shouted as the rain tried to drown out their voices. "This holiday has opened me up to acquire this brand-new talent of mine!"

The she-devil cocked an eyebrow at him, still not believing her master.

He hiked his thumb over his shoulder and said with a grin," Okay, okay! There's a sign back there that confirms my claim! We are indeed in Portland."

"Lovely," the she-devil replied with a deadpan expression. "Which way is your next delivery?"

"I don't know yet." Lucifer said. "We need to get somewhere dry and out of the rain. I don't want to ruin the letter."

"I think that it might flood here. If so…"

Lucifer glared at the she-devil and said, "Don't go there!"

Paroxysm leaned against the fallen angel and put her head on his shoulder with the biggest grin that she could muster as she finally said with glee, "I *Noah* guy, sire!"

Lucifer rolled his eyes and groaned loudly, "Cute, Paroxysm. Very cute. Now, be helpful and find us a place to go before a bloody whale shows up to swallow us whole!"

The she-devil glanced around and saw an overpass down the road from them, "Let's use the bridge for a bit so you can get your bearings."

Lucifer nodded as they both hurried over to find shelter from the deluge from above. The underpass was covered in graffiti and refuse. Several homeless people were huddled together next to a makeshift tent that utilized several tarps and shopping charts.

The people looked at the duo from Hell and bowed their heads respectfully. Lucifer dried off his hands as he asked, "Are you keeping your vessels warm?"

"Yes, sire." An elderly woman responded as her eyes turned black. "This one is old but she tends to abscond from that facility over there by the coffee shop. Maggie tells me that it's a nightmare living arrangement so she runs off just for her own freedom. She was almost dead before I got to her."

"I see." The fallen angel replied as he pulled out the envelope and scanned the area, but then something caught his attention. He looked back at the envelope and examined the handwriting. One thing stood out was that it had been written by an adult.

The fallen angel felt like the owner of the wish was somewhere in a large facility that sat next to a coffee shop.

He turned and showed the demon and asked, "Do you recognize the address?"

The elderly possessed woman eyed it closely and said, "Yes, sire. It's the same place that Maggie keeps escaping from."

"Are there any children in there?" Lucifer asked, wondering why an adult would write a letter to him.

The demon thought for a moment before saying, "Only one, sire. The rest are adults, either elderly or trying to recover from some form of trauma to their bodies."

Lucifer nodded as he pulled out the letter. The writing was done by the same person, though it had a few words with letters jumbled in the wish.

"This is a strange one," Lucifer commented.

"How so?" Paroxysm asked as looked at him, hoping for an explanation.

"It's a child's wish, written by an adult, that resides in a convalescent home." The fallen angel replied with a puzzled look on his angelic visage as he put the letter back into the envelope.

He slipped it back into his pocket and motioned to the she-devil to follow him to the facility. Lucifer didn't fully read the wish but he definitely wanted an answer for this one.

The rain seemed to come down harder, causing the street to flood from the nonstop onslaught. Water splashed with each step that the duo from Hell took.

Lucifer pulled on the entrance door but it didn't budge. He groaned as he gave it a swift yank, dislodging it from the magnetic locks at the top of the door frame.

They strolled in, shaking the excessive amounts of water from their clothes in a small vestibule. As Lucifer opened a glass door, a little buzzing alarm went off. Several attendants and a female nurse came running around the corner, expecting to find someone trying to leave the building.

They all halted when they saw the duo from Hell and looked at one another.

The nurse asked with a gruff voice, "Who are you two and how did you get in here?"

Lucifer motioned behind him, "Through the front door, obviously. My name is Lucifer and this striking young lady is Paroxysm. We're here to see Amanda. Is she awake?"

"Visiting hours aren't for another five hours," the nurse replied as she pointed at the front door. "You both need to leave, right now!"

"It's not like any of you can make us leave," Lucifer said with a bored expression as he pulled out the envelope. "And yet, everyone tonight has had that same idea."

"You're right, that's why we call the police." One of the attendants retorted as he pulled out his phone.

Paroxysm walked over to the attendant and snatched his phone from his hand. She eyed the angry man as she shattered the phone with a simple squeeze from her devilish grip.

The she-devil let the pieces fall harmlessly to the carpeted floor and snarked, "That's how you reach out and touch someone." She revealed her razor-sharp teeth and made her black eyes pulsate as she threatened the men as her claws extended, "Now, leave before I do the same to both of you! If I discover that either of you call the police and interrupt the will of Hell, I'll slowly peel off your faces slowly."

The attendants both screamed as they fled, leaving the nurse behind. She was about to turn and run too but Paroxysm grabbed the woman and kept her in place. The nurse protested as she tried to free herself from Paroxysm's grip but nothing worked.

"Let me go, damnit!" The nurse cried out, pleading with her captors. "I don't have any money or anything that you might want!"

The she-devil whispered in the nurse's ear seductively, "We only here to make a delivery to a child. Play your cards right and I'll give you such pleasure that you'll feel like it's a form of torture."

"Paroxysm, don't frighten the poor mortal with a good time. She has a job to do, much like we do tonight." The fallen angel admonished her. Lucifer looked at the envelope and then back at the nurse and stated, "You're the one that wrote Amanda's Christmas wish to me, aren't you?"

"What?" The nurse looked at Lucifer as she furrowed her brow. "I don't understand."

He walked over to her and handed the envelope to her. She gasped when she recognized it and added, "Where did you get this? You shouldn't have it. It's supposed to go to Santa. You don't look like that jolly old man."

"That's an astute observation, Mrs," the fallen angel looked at her badge, "Olivia. Do tell me why you wrote this for little Amanda in the first place?"

"It would be best if I showed you but keep your friend from molesting me," Olivia said as Paroxysm flicked her tongue lightly on her ear, causing the nurse to shutter.

"Let the woman go." Lucifer ordered as his eyes glowed with a sigh.

"Your loss." The she-devil murmured as she grazed Olivia's ass before stepping away. "You don't know what you're missing out on, Olivia."

The nurse rubbed her arm and asked warily, "What are you two?"

"I told you that I'm Lucifer. The Devil himself. Paroxysm is one of my she-devils whose sole purpose is to torture the wicked souls that come to Hell. You put my name on the envelope and I got it. Why did you do that?"

Olivia blushed slightly, "I have dyslexia so I jumble letters in words at times. I had to dictate the letter for Amanda. Her room is this way. Follow me and please don't make any more trouble for me. My boss is already looking for a reason to get rid of me."

They all walked through the reception area and took a left down long hallway. The air in the facility smelled of sterilizing chemicals mixed with a barely pungent aroma of urine, feces, and a hint of death.

The she-devil walked next to the nurse and asked, "Why does your boss want to get rid of you?"

"He's a prick that believes that he's better than all of us. To him, I'm not worth keeping around because of my dyslexia and other health issues. He's said as much. I've almost quit on numerous occasions because he won't staff us at night properly but when Amanda arrived, I chose to stay and endure the abuse because she needs the care. We're short staffed because of Bill so the ones that suffer more than me are the residents here. Those two guys that you scared are the only help I have here. This place is a nightmare and a living Hell for everyone, except for Bill."

"Sounds like someone should pay the man a visit." Lucifer said as he looked at the she-devil. "Is he here now?"

Olivia snorted, "Fuck no! He's on a vacation down in Mexico and won't be back until the first of February."

"Is Amanda's word usage that horrid?" Paroxysm asked.

"No. I'm sure that her handwriting would be nicer than mine," the nurse said as they turned right down a shorter hallway. "You'll understand more when we get to her room."

Lucifer noticed that the nurse had a small tattoo on the back of her neck of the triple moon so he asked, "My dear, are you pagan?"

Olivia warily looked at the fallen angel and said, "Yes. Is there a problem with that?"

"No, I was just curious since I can see that you have that tattoo. Does that path make you happy?" Lucifer asked.

"It beats being told to be good or you will burn in Hell. I believe that there are more than just one god, other than your Father, because I've interacted more with them. No offense, but I never believed in you and what the Christians have been peddling." The nurse shrugged her shoulders.

"None taken. Humanity is to blame for that. Control the masses, use my Father as their weapon of righteousness, and have me be the ultimate punishment if folks didn't follow their rules. Frankly, if people do good, then they will be fine. If they do bad, then I get them. Quite simple really and yet, humans have to go make it all complicated. I don't have any issues with what you believe in, just be true to yourself and others."

"Trust me, Olivia," Paroxysm added as she put a hand on the nurse's shoulder. "People do enough terrible acts that they keep me and the other devils busy for several lifetimes whether they believe in Hell or not."

Olivia stopped at a door and said calmly with a hint of sadness, "This is Amanda's room. Let's see if she's up for a little company tonight."

The nurse lightly knocked on the door as she opened it. The room was mostly dark, the only light coming from the various medical devices next to the bed where a ten-year-old child lay quietly. Amanda barely opened her eyes, looking frail and weak. A breathing tube snaked down in her throat, helping the little girl with her respirations. Her body was covered in a light blue fuzzy blanket, where numerous wires could be seen at the edges of it.

Both Lucifer and the she-devil gasped at the sight of the child. An electronic humming filled the room as a blood pressure machine activated next to Amanda. She stared at the people in her room with vacant eyes.

"What has happened to this child?" Paroxysm demanded.

Olivia walked over and sat down in a chair by Amanda's bed. She reached out and took the child by her hand and said, "A tragic car accident. She and her parents were heading to see friends for Thanksgiving when her car got hit by a drunk driver on I-5. The truck was in their lane, going the wrong way, and hit her parent's car, doing at least one hundred and ten miles an hour. Amanda has had several surgical procedures but nothing helped her. She's now a quadriplegic. Only a week ago, she could talk but her ability to breathe has deteriorated to the point of needing mechanical assistance. Before that, Amanda had me write the letter that you got.

This is her life now and will be for however long it will last."

Lucifer walked over to the opposite side of the bed. He looked down at the child and said, "Amanda, I'm not Santa but I'm here because your nurse mailed your cryptic Christmas wish to me. My name is Lucifer so if I'm to grant your wish, we need to talk."

The nurse pointed at the girl, "Amanda can't speak with that tube–"

"I'm well aware of that, Olivia." Lucifer cut her off. He looked at the child and said, "You can speak directly to me using your mental voice in your head. I'll be able to hear you if you can focus on me. Can you give it a try, Amanda?"

Amanda blinked several times at the fallen angel before mentally replying, "*I think that I'm doing this right. I don't know if you can hear me.*"

Lucifer smiled benevolently, "I heard you just fine, little one. I'll talk out loud so that you can have confirmation. Now, what is it that you want for Christmas, Amanda?"

"I'm not sure that what I want is something that you can do. Don't be mad at me for asking." Amanda replied as her eyes welled up with tears.

The ruler of Hell furrowed his brow, "If your desire is to walk once more, I'm afraid that is something beyond my skills. If I could do it, I would do it in a heartbeat."

"*Oh,*" Amanda said as she looked down, blinking her eyes as her tears spilled out. "*Can you take away pain? Everything hurts. The medicine doesn't help as much anymore.*"

"That falls under the same as what I said that I can't do." Lucifer replied as he sat down on the bed, pondering what he could do for this child.

"What does she want, sire?" Paroxysm asked, "Do you need me to go get something for her?"

"She wants her pain to go away. I don't know how to accomplish that." The fallen angel said as he crossed his arms across his chest.

"Ask Olivia. She knows what I want." Amanda said as she rapidly blinked her eyes.

Lucifer looked at the nurse and asked, "What does she want? Amanda told me that you already know."

Olivia squeezed Amanda's hand and asked sadly, "Are you sure that this is what you want? We talked about it but are you truly ready?"

Amanda grimaced as she looked at the nurse. She nodded slightly before returning her attention to the fallen angel.

"Euthanasia. That's what Amanda wants." Olivia informed the duo from Hell.

"She wants to die?" The she-devil gasped. She hurried over to the child and got close to her face; concern etched on her demonic visage. "Is there nothing else that you desire? Surely, we can figure out something better than death."

"Besides the obvious," Lucifer motioned his arm over Amanda's prone body, "how did a nine-year-old child get the idea of suicide in the first place?"

Olivia let go of Amanda's hand and stood up. She paced back and forth with her arms wrapped around her chest and explained, "One day, I was in here taking care of Amanda when a lengthy documentary played on the TV about Dr Jack Kevorkian. She became fascinated by the doctor and his work in assisted suicide. Amanda asked a lot of questions about it and I did my best to dissuade her from thinking about it but she wouldn't let it go. A few days before she lost her ability to speak, Amanda became adamant about wanting to end her suffering. I wish that I could do it but I'd get thrown in prison for it."

Lucifer tapped a finger on his chin, "I don't like the idea of killing a child. It's not right, but I can also see it from Amanda's perspective. I can tell that she doesn't have long to live so I suppose I can ask for an expert on what to do."

The nurse paused. She looked at the ruler of Hell as he closed his eyes, softly chanting, and asked him, "And who's this *expert*?"

A cold blast of air swept into the room, causing Olivia to shiver. A dark shape manifested slowly next to Lucifer. The she-devil eyes went black as they pulsated, her claws extended as she prepared to defend the fallen angel.

Lucifer put his hand up and shook his head at Paroxysm and reassured her, "Stand down, Paroxysm. It's just a reaper answering my call."

The dark shape coalesced into a more humanoid form. The reaper wore a black robe as dark as obsidian and nothing else. Its visage was taut to the point of seeing every curve of its skull, the skin was a shiny ebony with pure white glowing eyes.

The reaper looked at Amanda first for a moment before turning its head to Lucifer and asked with a raspy voice, "It isn't her time to go. I can't take her."

"I understand that much." Lucifer said with a hint of irritation. "What can we do to help ease her suffering?"

"In order for that to occur, one of you must end her mortal existence." The reaper said matter of fact.

"I don't like this, sire." Paroxysm grumbled as she furrowed her brow. "It doesn't seem right."

"I'm in agreement with you, but this is her Christmas wish." Lucifer nodded with a sigh. He looked down at the child and asked, "Are you sure that this is what you desire?"

"*Yes, but does this mean that I'll be going to Hell for killing myself?*" Amanda asked as grimaced in pain.

"No, my dear. Contrary to what you mortals believe, suicide doesn't get one sent to Hell. It is the choice to end the suffering that can no longer be tolerated. It's not a cowardly act or simply taking the easy way out. It takes a great deal of courage to set your foot down and say 'no more'. Human existence is nothing but pain and suffering, one that gets perpetuated with guilt and shame. I guarantee that you will be with your parents when I fulfill your Christmas wish."

Amanda's eyes widened with excitement, *"So, you're really going to do it? I'll be with my parents after I die?"*

The fallen angel had a look of disgust, "I detest killing you but a wish is a wish, I suppose." He eyed the reaper as he added, "I'm fairly certain that you will be reunited with them."

"I shall see to it that Amanda is reunited. So, how do you plan on fulfilling your end of this deal, Lucifer?" The reaper stated.

Lucifer looked at both Paroxysm and the nurse and ordered, "Both of you leave the room."

Olivia protested, "But, I'd like to be here for–"

"No, you won't." The ruler of Hell cut her off. "Olivia, it's sweet that you want to be here for her demise but you can't be. If you want to be blamed for her death, then stay. The authorities will see to it that you pay for her death. Paroxysm, please escort her from the room."

"Yes, sire." The she-devil replied as she took Olivia by her arm but then she paused and let go of her.

Paroxysm leaned down over the child and gently kissed her on the forehead and said, "I would say be brave but you already are. May you find peace when this is done, Amanda."

The fallen angel cleared his throat as he pointed at the door. The she-devil took Olivia by her arm once again and ushered her out of the room. The reaper floated over next to Lucifer, its ethereal form would fade in and out of existence at times.

"What method have you chosen?" The reaper asked, devoid of any emotions.

"I'm not sure. I have a few options but I want this to appear to be accidental." The fallen angel replied. He looked at the tubing in Amanda's mouth, debating on pulling it out but that would raise suspicion. Another thought was to unplug it but he dismissed it.

Lucifer looked out the window and saw that the rain was still pouring down. Every so often, a flash of lightning brightened the sky. He walked over to the breathing machine and grabbed the cord. The fallen angel's eyes glowed brightly as he sent a surge of energy through it, causing the machine to malfunction. He looked over at Amanda and saw a single tear trickle down her cheek.

The fear that showed in her eyes slowly dissipated as the reaper hovered over her. It reached inside Amanda's little body and gently pulled out her spirit. She had a look of uncertainty but then Amanda smiled.

"I don't hurt no more!" The child cried out happily.

"I'm glad to hear that," Lucifer replied as he dropped the power cord, not feeling as jovial about Amanda's situation.

He felt a cold embrace from behind. Lucifer looked down and saw Amanda hugging him around his waist.

He glanced up at the reaper and it only said, "She requested this; to thank you."

"Odd thing to hug your killer," the fallen angel grimaced as he felt uncomfortable and uncertain how to accept this.

Amanda let go of Lucifer and said, "Thanks for granting my wish! Now, I get to go be with my parents! Be good, devil man!"

The reaper took Amanda and they both disappeared from the room, leaving the ruler of Hell all alone. He marched out of the room and made his way to the nurses' station where Olivia and the she-devil sat.

"Is–" the nurse stammered, "is Amanda gone?"

"Amanda is where she needs to be and is no longer in pain," Lucifer replied as he shook his slightly.

Olivia held her hands over her face and sobbed. Paroxysm sat on top of the table, rubbing the woman's back. She looked at Lucifer and asked with genuine concern, "Are you okay, sire?"

"Not particularly, no. I don't make it a habit of killing innocent children. Mark me, Paroxysm: Rabbit *will not* have a pleasant experience when I have that damn trickster in my realm." Lucifer replied gruffly. He adjusted his jacket and vest and asked the nurse, "Right. Now then, Olivia, what is *your* Christmas wish?"

The nurse blew her nose and wiped the tears from her eyes and said, "Huh? What do you mean by that?"

"Yes, now I'm curious to know." Paroxysm asked as she kept stroking Olivia's back.

"The wish was from Amanda but you, Olivia, composed it for her. That means that you get a Christmas gift from the Devil himself."

"What would you like, my dear?" The she-devil asked as she slipped off the desktop and stood behind the nurse. She gently massaged Olivia's shoulders as she added, "What does a woman like you want tonight?"

"I don't know. I can't think of anything. I'm not sure if I deserve a gift." Olivia answered.

"I'd smite your boss but I feel like he's going to have a difficult time explaining Amanda's death, especially since it happened due to some faulty wiring and negligent building upkeep." The fallen angel stated as he placed his hands on the tabletop, looking directly at the nurse, "Do tell Satan Claws what you desire."

Olivia thought about it for a moment before saying, "My wish is for both of you to be happy and feel loved."

Paroxysm paused her massaging, freezing in place with a stunned visage. Lucifer's mouth gaped open as he kept throwing looks between the nurse and the she-devil.

"I'm not sure if I can fulfill that request," Lucifer replied, trying to understand her wish.

Olivia stood up and pointed at the ruler of Hell and yelled, "This whole problem is *my* fault! If I hadn't written the letter, you wouldn't be racked with guilt from pulling the plug on Amanda!"

"Shorted out the machine actually, but that's just semantics at this point." Lucifer retorted.

Olivia turned around and motioned to the she-devil and said, "And you, Paroxysm, I can tell that this has affected you so much that you take solace by touching another person."

"I–I never thought about it like that." Paroxysm stammered slightly. "I'm a hands-on kind of devil, which is why I enjoy torturing damned souls. I'm great at what I do but I've never had to contend with this kind of experience like tonight."

The nurse walked around the reception table towards Lucifer. She dropped down on her knees, hung her head, and said, "Then I wish that you would take me to Hell and torture me for causing both of you so much grief. You can have her do her worst to me."

"You are a strange person, you know that?" Lucifer replied as he shook his head. "Why are you so willing to throw yourself down into the pit?"

"Because the guilt and grief is getting to be too much for me to bear. I loved that little girl! Amanda deserved a better life than what got handed to her! Watching her slowly die was heartbreaking and now that she's dead, I feel like I'm responsible."

"Well, I must say that you're one of the few mortals that actually takes responsibility for your own actions and not blaming me or my Father for everything that goes wrong." Lucifer said as he rubbed his chin thoughtfully. "Is it truly your desire to go to Hell?"

As Olivia nodded solemnly, Paroxysm rushed over and possessively grabbed the nurse and squealed with a grin, "Can she? I promise that I'll take care of her! I'll feed her and take her for daily walks! I'm sure that Olivia is housebroken, sire!" The she-devil lost all merriment as she added, "I'll torture her if that is what you want, Lucifer."

Lucifer pinched the bridge of his nose, shaking his head, "Dear Father, what have I gotten myself into? I'll be so happy when this damn holiday is done! Will this night never end?"

Paroxysm got up and leaned into the fallen angel and said coyly, "You love me and you know it, sire." Lucifer glared down at her as the she-devil made a pouty face and added, "I'll keep her safe or torture her, it's your choice, but I hope that you don't choose the latter."

"Will you stop that, you're making a scene in front of your new *pet*!" Lucifer groaned, causing Paroxysm to giggle. He looked down at Olivia and asked, "It's actually up to you. What do you want? Torture or be a personal companion to Paroxysm?"

Olivia stood up and said, "Why are you giving me a choice?"

"Because everyone has a choice." Lucifer explained. "I don't mind you being in my realm but you need to be there of your own free will, since you're not dead. My Father gave you free will for a reason, so make your choice, please. I have one more stop to make and we're running out of time."

The nurse thought about it for a moment. She looked over at the she-devil and saw that Paroxysm had turned her back to her. Olivia walked up to her and wrapped her arms around her and said, "I've made my choice."

"Splendid! Which one? She's going to be either your demise or your desire so hugging Paroxysm is leaving this open to interpretation."

"Fine," Olivia walked around to face the she-devil. She noticed that Paroxysm's eyes were darting around anxiously. The nurse smiled as she leaned forward and pressed her lips against hers, eliciting a squeal of delight from the she-devil.

Olivia pulled away to speak to the fallen angel with a smirk, "Does that answer your question or should I go further so this isn't open to interpretation?"

Paroxysm bit her bottom lip, "I vote for going further. I do love the way that you choose, Olivia."

"Very well, but Paroxysm, you will have to see to her every need and make sure that she remains safe. Am I clear? If she dies because you don't make it abundantly clear to the other denizens of Hell that Olivia is off limits, that's on you."

"Then I'll mark her as my familiar and make a formal declaration that if anyone tries *anything,* I'll place them on my table." Paroxysm stated.

She used one of her black claws and nicked her finger. Olivia held out her hand and let the she-devil cut her finger. Paroxysm held their bloody hands together as she placed her other hand on the nurse's face and proclaimed, "I take this mortal before me as my willing familiar to protect and mark her as my *lover*!"

"I accept your terms, Paroxysm." Olivia said with a warm smile.

"Paroxysm, take her home. I believe that I can handle the final wish on my own." Lucifer ordered as he pulled out the last envelope. He glanced at them and added, "I recognize your oath to her and place my mark on Olivia."

The nurse grunted as she felt a burning sensation on her forehead. She reached up and rubbed it, hoping to alleviate the pain.

Paroxysm pressed her lips against her forehead and said, "Don't fret, Olivia. Lucifer branded you with his mark because he's a sweet little devil. Now no one will bother you unless they want to incur mine and his wrath."

"Oh please," Lucifer said as he opened up a portal. "Get a torture room already! Your wish has been granted, Olivia. Enjoy your stay in Hell."

The she-devil wrapped her arms around her new familiar and vanished just as Lucifer stepped through the portal.

Chapter Fourteen

Don't Mess With Me

Lucifer stepped out of the portal and saw that he was in a rundown part of a small town. He looked up at the sky and saw the sun shining brightly.

Christmas day.

The fallen angel pulled out the envelope and scanned the area for his final delivery. He noticed that this child seemed to be on the move. Lucifer felt it would be best to fly around and hunt for the kid, using the thick clouds as cover. He was just about to take to the sky when a big red sleigh landed next to him.

Santa stepped out of his magical ride, glaring at the fallen angel.

"Well, if it isn't the jolly fat man himself!" Lucifer jovially called out. "Still have a few last-minute gifts to hand out before you take a year off?"

Santa poked the fallen angel on his chest as he admonished, "I finished with all of my presents! You, on the other hand, have delivered nothing but misery and chaos! What do you have to say about it?"

"I was pretty efficient, if you ask me." Lucifer replied, grinning ear to ear. He swatted Santa's hand away and asked, "What's got your jingle bells in a twist?"

Santa shook his head in disgust, "You've made a mockery of this joyous holiday. Why couldn't you just hand over the bag and let me do it?"

Lucifer lost all traces of humor as he crossed his arms over his chest, "Those weren't meant for you, remember? They wanted Satan, not Santa. They made a deal with the Devil and I deliver on whatever the little urchins wanted, much like you do."

"I don't leave death and destruction in my wake! You have single-handedly ruined Christmas!"

"Now, you're being a drama queen." Lucifer replied dismissively, "What I granted tonight is beyond your skills so, in a sense, I outdid you on this festive night."

"Thousands slaughtered? A child burning down a town?" Santa shouted incredulously. "How could you allow this to happen?"

Lucifer chuckled, "Ah, Chad Masterson! I imagine that he's on your naughty list? In my defense, I was going by *your* guidelines for the holiday."

"I never said for you to kill so many innocent people!"

"I gave them what they asked for, or at least something close to it since it can vary. Those are the words that you used to explain the gift giving process. A child wanted world peace so I had all those in powerful positions killed."

"That's barbaric, even for you!" Santa grumbled in disgust.

"Problem solving at its finest is what I'd call it." Lucifer replied with a smirk. "Now, if you're quite finished crying over the spilled milk and cookies, I have one final delivery to make."

"It's Christmas day, your deliveries are over!" Santa stated as he pointed at the ground, "You failed! Go back to Hell where you belong. You lost your wager to the trickster, much like a certain golden fiddle."

The fallen angel backhanded Santa across his chubby, rosy red cheek, "Bring that up again and I'll tear your ho ho ho bits off and shove them down your throat, fat man!"

Lucifer grunted as several volleys of ice arrows struck him in his chest. He glared menacingly at the small army of ice elves as they notched more arrows.

"So be it, Santa. You want a war, then you'll have it." The ruler of Hell coldly remarked as he melted the arrows from his body. Lucifer lifted himself up in the air with his white eyes blazing as he spoke in Enochian.

"Stand down!" Santa frantically cried out, "Stand down now!"

The ground shook violently as the earth fractured open. Searing heat emanated from the fissure as the denizens from Hell crawled out. Ice arrows flew towards the fissure as

Santa's elves tried to repel the many creatures coming to the surface.

"Call back your monsters, Lucifer!" Santa called out, "Innocent people could die from this skirmish!"

"You brought your minions to kill me. It's only fair that I return the favor." Lucifer retorted coldly, not caring about the carnage that his minions would create. He landed back on the ground and punched Santa in his bulbous gut.

Lucifer chuckled as Santa staggered backwards, "The poem is correct about you. Your belly feels like a bowl full of jelly."

Santa roared as he created a festive sword that resembled a candy cane with a green bow as a guard. He slashed at Lucifer, cutting him across his chest.

Santa maniacally laughed as he taunted the fallen angel by pointing his sword at the blow he just landed, "Now you'll learn why they refer to me as Saint *Nick*!"

Lucifer glared as he brandished his own sword. The blade glowed brightly as a white flame danced on it as he retorted, "A Nick won't kill me. I'll be sure to show you how it's done. This will be the day the damn Christmas music dies. Engarde, fat man!"

Scream rang in the air as demons of all sizes and levels tore through the army of ice elves. Many of them scattered, trying to find a better defensive position to launch their volleys.

Lucifer effortlessly blocked each blow from Santa. He parried with several slashing arches and thrusts, pushing Santa back. He held his festive weapon with both hands as sweat glistened over his skin.

"Santa!" One elf cried out as several demons encroached on her, "Help us!"

Santa couldn't help but glance over to see who was calling to him. To his horror, Santa could only watch as the female ice elf was ripped apart and devoured. Lucifer stepped up next to Santa and grabbed both of his arms. With one fluid cleave, the fallen angel chopped off Santa's hands at his wrists, the scorching hot blade cut through with little resistance.

Santa groaned loudly as he dropped to his knees as the shock from his cauterized wounds took hold. Lucifer turned him around, forcing the jolly man to watch the battle as he hissed coldly, "Look what you did by bringing your pathetic army here. Elves verses demons. It's a fitting scene as old as time, albeit this one is a one-sided fight."

Fires burned all around, vehicles were covered in ash and gore. Bodies from both sides littered the street. A small group of the remaining elves had been disarmed and were being toyed with by the demonic forces that surrounded them.

"Spare them! They're unarmed and no longer a threat." Santa pleaded to the ruler of Hell. "Let them flee in peace."

"Mercy is an attribute that I don't possess in battle. Don't fret, your little warriors aren't going to die just yet. As you can see," Lucifer sheathed his sword and then pointed as each elf had vicious claws piercing their bodies as the demons dragged them forcefully back to the fissure. "they're going to be honorary guests in my domain."

"You should *never* have been allowed to live." Santa said with a shaky voice, "Hell was never the perfect punishment for you, Lucifer!"

The fallen angel spun Santa around to face him. He roughly grabbed the jolly man by his face as he sneered, "You know nothing about punishment. You judge all the little girls and boys and decide who gets gifts and who gets heartache. Now, it's your turn to learn what happens to all those naughty elves of yours. You will not enjoy your stay in Hell because, like them, this trip will be my Christmas present to all of you! Take him away, behemoth!"

Santa cried out as the monstrous beast sank its claws into his blubbery flesh. It effortlessly lifted Santa up like he weighed less than a feather as it trudged towards the fissure.

Lucifer adjusted his jacket and vest. He picked up the jolly man's hands and candy cane sword and marched over to the fissure. Several demons kneeled before him as he ordered, "Put this sword in my throne room and take Santa's hands and feed them to him."

"Yes, sire!" The demons said in unison as they took the items from him and hurried down into the fissure.

Lucifer chanted softly in Enochian, forcing the fissure to seal back up. He unfurled his tendril wings and took to the sky. He searched the area closest to the boy's last location before he got distracted by the battle. Still no visual sign of him but there were traces of the kid's signature. It was erratic and all over the place, like the boy was playing hide and seek on a grand scale.

"Where are you, little urchin?" Lucifer muttered out loud to himself.

As he made his way further into the town, the signature grew stronger. The fallen angel spotted a large school and with it, his intended target. Lucifer noticed a cluster of kids gathering around a metal and wooden jungle gym, laughing like crazed hyenas.

The older group of kids were throwing snowballs at one child that was dangling from one of the monkey bar rungs.

Lucifer grabbed the envelope and realized that the child being tormented was his final delivery.

As he streaked down towards the playground, Lucifer commented, "I guess that I have to save the day yet again."

He landed twenty feet away from the group quietly and marched towards them as he adjusted his jacket and vest. The fallen angel could hear a lot of taunting and name calling coming from the group.

"You thought that you could hide from us? Man, you should know better than to run from us, Hunter!" One of the kids shouted as the others took great delight in pelting Hunter with more snowballs.

"You know that we like you, Hunter," another kid said with a chuckle. "This hurts us more than it will ever hurt you."

"Please," Hunter sobbed as his little body spun around painfully, the nylon ropes that were used to hoist him up were cutting into his skin. His wrists and feet were hogtied together, making it difficult to avoid the volley of snowballs. "Stop it! This hurts! I'm going to be sick!"

"Don't be such a big baby!" A girl called out as she hit him in the mouth with her snowball just as Hunter lost the contents of his stomach. "Hey, look guys! Hunter has made a barf slushy!"

Everyone laughed as one boy started chanting, "Lick it up! Lick it up! Lick it up!"

As Hunter pushed his tongue out past his swollen lips, Lucifer commanded with a booming voice, "Don't even think about licking your face, Hunter! All of you brats leave *now*!"

All the older kids turned around to look at the fallen angel. Several sneered at him defiantly and flipped him off.

"Stay out of this, old man! This doesn't concern you!" One boy bellowed.

"Yeah, go back to the old folks home, grandpa!" Another boy added.

Lucifer coldly eyed them all and ordered, "Seven prepubescent pricks verses a five-year-old? Not very sporting of you. Release Hunter now!" He grinned maliciously as he added, "Or else…"

"Or else what, jackass?" One boy asked as he, along with the other older kids, threw snowballs at Lucifer. No matter how many they lobbed at him, the snowballs melted away, much to the children's astonishment.

The fallen angel chuckled, "Have none of you brats ever heard the expression *a snowball's chance in Hell*? Now, you know why it's not wise to attack the Devil himself."

Lucifer's eyes glowed brightly white as he summoned a small horde of demons. The older kids panicked and tried to run but were corralled by the denizens of Hell. The fallen angel walked past them and ordered, "If any of them try anything, peel off their skin like a banana."

The ruler of Hell ducked his head as he got close to Hunter and asked, "Let me guess: this is a daily occurrence?"

Hunter only sobbed in response. Lucifer reached out to untie the boy which caused Hunter to flinch.

"I'll take that as a yes." The fallen angel remarked as he pulled out the envelope and asked, "Is this your Christmas letter, Hunter Orenda?"

The little boy could barely see through his bleary eyes. He spoke softly, wincing as his lips split open, "I can't tell. Can't see good."

Lucifer nodded curtly as he said calmly, "Don't worry about it, Hunter. I know that you sent this Christmas wish to me. I'm going to get you down from here so that we can discuss your wish better. Would you like that, Hunter?"

Hunter grimaced as he nodded. Lucifer turned his head and ordered two of his demons, "Fetch a seat and a blanket."

"From Hell, sire?" A minor demon asked.

The fallen angel glared as he pointed at the closed school, "From there, you buffoon! Do you think that he needs something from our realm? Nevermind, don't answer. Just go, *now*!"

"Yes, Lucifer!" The minor demon called out as he fled towards the school.

Lucifer turned his attention back to Hunter and saw an upper-level demoness untying the boy. The demoness had brought several blankets and a big bean bag and had it sitting underneath Hunter.

Lucifer cocked his head curiously and stated, "At least someone knows what to do. I don't believe that you're one of my minions, who are you exactly and why are you here?"

"You are correct, Lucifer. I'm here for Hunter Orenda." The upper-level demoness responded as she gently sat the boy on the bean bag and threw several blankets around his shivering body. "My name is Lexx."

"What do you mean when you say that you're here for him?" The fallen angel narrowed his eyes with suspicion.

Lexx stepped back several feet with her hands up, "Nothing nefarious, if that's what troubles you. I'm not going to interfere with your task but I do request that I help him feel better."

"And how will you help Hunter? Do humor me, demoness."

"May I?" Lexx pointed at the boy. When the ruler of Hell nodded, the demoness stepped forward. She placed her hands on Hunter, which caused him to flinch unconsciously. She glanced at the fallen angel for a moment and then she chanted softly in her demonic language.

Lucifer was fascinated by the demoness as she used her magic to mend and heal Hunter's tiny body. The boy relaxed and smiled gingerly, unsure if his lips would hurt or not.

He looked at Lexx and said with a loving smile, "Thank you, strange lady!"

"You're an intriguing demoness, aren't you? I can see that you're using a glamor charm. Is that for Hunter's benefit?"

"No sense in traumatizing the boy any further than he already is, don't you agree?"

Lexx replied as she moved away. "I believe that he's ready to speak with you."

Lucifer nodded as he squatted down next to Hunter. He opened the envelope and pulled out the letter and read it to himself.

Hunter saw the envelope as clear as a spring day and said, "That's my letter! Are you Santa?"

"No, my dear boy." Lucifer merrily laughed, "Santa is all tied up at the moment so I'm here to grant your Christmas wish instead."

"So, he's real?" Hunter's eyes widened with delight.

"Oh yes, very much so." The fallen angel smirked, "We had a lengthy discussion earlier since your letter was the last one of the season. Santa was all tuckered out and is resting in my personal sauna so I took his hands off - I mean that I took *your letter* off his hands."

"I don't have any cookies and milk for him. Will he be mad at me?" Hunter asked with concern.

Lucifer dismissively replied with a grin, "Don't fret. Santa's getting his just desserts as we speak. Now, let's see what you want for Christmas, shall we?"

"I hope that it isn't asking for too much, sir." Hunter said as he fidgeted with his hands.

"Let's see," Lucifer read out loud. "You want something to keep me safe like an invisibility cloak so that you don't keep getting hurt." He glanced over at the detained children and added, "I believe that I understand why you would want something like that but why hide? They will eventually find you when you forget such an item. Besides, such an item doesn't exist."

"Perhaps something that he can use for the rest of his life, like a piece of jewelry or a talisman?" Lexx offered.

"Hunter needs to be able to stand up for himself if he's to learn to defend himself." The fallen angel eyed the demoness. "He can't have you fighting all of his battles for him."

"I can until he's ready. It's what I've been sent to do and then train Hunter to harness his abilities!" The demoness replied, not backing down from the ruler of Hell.

"What are you going on about? What do you mean by his abilities?" Lucifer asked as he eyed her.

"It has been foretold by many of our seerers that Hunter Orenda would be a force to be reckoned with and, in time, would either save many lives or extinguish them. Depending on his choices." Lexx explained.

Lucifer rolled his eyes with a huff, "Prophecies. Those are so overdone by everyone. My Father has a whole book devoted to such nonsense about me coming up here to enslave humanity and having an epic battle with his son. The truth of it is that humans don't need me to destroy this world, they are doing it all on their own without realizing it. I'll, of course, be blamed for everything because people can't take responsibility for their own destruction. If Jesus ever does return, he would either be committed to an asylum or killed by my Father's fanatical followers. Organized religion is like that. When people can't make sense of events or are searching for a purpose, they turn to religion for comfort. It's a trap that can twist the mind and control the masses. People will kill those that don't fit their beliefs, let alone their views of the world. Humanity is its own end of days, they just don't see it or choose blind ignorance."

"So, no cloak for me?" Hunter asked, feeling disappointed.

Lucifer kneeled down by the boy and reassured him, "Just because you can't have what you want doesn't mean that I can't grant you something better."

At that moment, a minor demon stumbled over to them, his feet all tangled up in the blanket that he found. It was damp in spots and dripping water as the demon held out the blanket to the ruler of Hell.

Lucifer eyed his minion and flatly asked with a deadpan expression, "Is it your notion that I wrap Hunter in the warm, loving embrace of hypothermia?"

"What? No, sire! I wouldn't do–"

"Get out of my sight before I make you disappear. *Permanently*!" Lucifer threatened as his eyes glowed brightly.

The minor demon fled, dropping the wet blanket in the process. The fallen angel shook his head as he turned to Lexx and said, "I need to go grab his gift, will you keep Hunter company?"

"I would do it whether you want me to or not," the demoness replied as she placed a hand on the boy's shoulder protectively.

Lucifer nodded curtly as he vanished. The demoness saw that Hunter's gaze was transfixed on the denizens of Hell that had his older tormentors huddled together. Each demon took delight in throwing snowballs at them and menacing each bully.

"Why aren't you hurting me like them?" Hunter asked, still watching the demonic spectacle.

"Why would you believe that I want to harm a single hair on your head?" Lexx replied as she stroked her fingers through his dark curly hair.

"Everyone does eventually." Hunter said flatly.

"I'm not like those people that went out of their way to hurt you," the demoness did her best to placate his fears.

He pointed at the group and said, "But shouldn't you be doing that to me? You look similar to those monsters over there."

Lexx looked surprised at the boy's declaration as the fallen angel reappeared. He looked at the demoness and then Hunter as he came over to them.

"What did I miss? Lexx, you look like you just downed a bottle of holy water." Lucifer asked.

"She looked just like those monsters over there," Hunter answered. He looked up at the demoness and added, "Why do you look like a person and a monster?"

"Hmmm," the fallen angel commented out loud, "sounds like the boy has the sight and can see through your disguise. Does Lexx frighten you, Hunter?"

Lexx had a glimmer of fear cross her demonic visage as she waited for the boy's answer.

Hunter couldn't take his eyes off the demoness as he spoke, "Both. I'm not sure why but I do and don't. Those things over there frighten me more than she does, though. Does that count for something?"

As Lexx relaxed, Lucifer answered as he spoke like a professor to a student, "It does. Demons cause people fear and do many terrible things that can make a person feel bad. Lexx is a demon, like those over by your *friends*, but she's different from them. She may very well be one that you can trust but not fully because demons can have ulterior motives. I'm not sure what her purpose is so use your best judgment and follow your instincts. That said, hold out your right hand, Hunter."

The boy eagerly did as he was asked, excited to see his gift. He watched on with anticipation as Lucifer pulled out a shiny object from his jacket pocket. Hunter seemed mesmerized by it as it glinted in the sunlight.

It was a silver ring that had a blood ruby and a cobalt sapphire in the center of a pentagram. Sigils were etched along the band that pulsated at times.

"This ring will keep you protected from those that wish to do you harm. It does this by glowing, which indicates the intentions of the individual. Red for bad and blue for good." Lucifer explained. He pulled out a small needle and added, "In order to activate it, the ring requires a drop of your blood. Just a pin prick on one of your fingers, that's all. It won't hurt but a moment."

Hunter stuck his index finger out and said with a shrug, "Go ahead, I'm used to pain so I'm not worried about it."

The fallen angel took Hunter's hand and jabbed his finger quickly, barely causing the boy to flinch. He squeezed the finger to coax the blood out and touched the ring against it. To Hunter's amazement, the ring seemed to soak up the blood like it was drinking water and somehow alive. The sigils along the band glowed brightly and the pentagram pulsated before going dormant.

Hunter put the ring on his right index finger. It seemed too big for him to wear but to Hunter's surprise, it shrank down and fit perfectly.

"Okay, Hunter, here's the rules for the ring. Only you can wear it because it's bonded to you. If someone else tries it on, it will cause them immense pain. As I said before, the gems will glow and let you know a person's intentions towards you but only you can see it when it happens."

Hunter pointed the ring at Lucifer and then towards Lexx. He felt confused about it and asked, "What does it mean when both gems glow at the same time?"

"It simply means that the person is in the middle. Meaning that they are neither good or bad but have the potential to go either way, depending on their choices. It's best to be cautious around them." Lucifer explained.

"I see." The boy nodded as he pointed it at the demons and their captives. The blood ruby glowed and never once did the sapphire light up. He looked up at the fallen angel and said, "Thank you for the gift. I will take good care of it."

Lucifer smiled as he patted Hunter on his head. He looked at the demoness and said, "Do what you must with miscreants over there. I'll be taking my minions back now."

"I plan on making each one fear the idea of coming after Hunter Orenda ever again." Lexx replied as she put her hands on the boy's shoulders.

Lucifer nodded as he turned to look at his demons and ordered, "Time to go. You have better things to do down in Hell than play with these brats."

One by one, the demons vanished as the ruler of Hell walked over to the cowering bullies, his eyes blazing white with his tendril wings out on display. Lucifer remarked coldly, "Keep doing what you've been doing and I'll be seeing each of you in Hell before you know it. Trust me, there won't be snowballs used to torture you. Got it?"

Each kid nodded as they cowered, crying as Lucifer disappeared before their eyes. They looked over at Hunter and fled in terror as Lexx dropped her glamour, revealing her true form as she ran a clawed finger across her throat as she glared at them.

Chapter Fifteen

A Rabbit's Tale

Lucifer sat down on his black marble throne with his fingers steepled under his chin. He thought about his little excursion to Earth, wondering if it was actually worth it or not.

A deal is a deal. I had no choice in the matter. So why do I feel like I should have done more?

The ruler of Hell observed what transpired with his minions during the holiday, using his blood scrying pool before him. It felt like every child had gotten what they asked for, within reason that is, and yet Lucifer was troubled by something.

"What am I missing?" He said to himself out loud. Lucifer focused on the signature of the trickster so that he could see the one that caused all of this chaos in the first place and how it did it.

Rabbit appeared as a lovely woman, beguiling her way into each post office and placing a small red plastic container at each location. He observed her whispering a magical incantation over each one, causing the sigils on the container to glow from her spell work.

"Clever little minx," Lucifer commented as he saw her shift into a rabbit and dart off to the next location. "I can't wait to finally meet you."

Ever since he returned to Hell, the fallen angel tried to locate her but it seemed that Rabbit was jumping from one interdimensional realm to the next. Rabbit was on the run because of the sizable bounty that Lucifer placed on her furry little head. It didn't help that the trickster was using her magical prowess to block her whereabouts, which infuriated the ruler of Hell.

Lucifer stood up and waved his hand over the blood pool to dispel it. He paced around his throne room, fuming that he didn't have Rabbit yet.

"How can one trickster be so damn elusive?" Lucifer muttered.

He walked over to the wall where he had one of the politicians that was killed on

Christmas Eve by his minions. The man had been stripped of his clothes and chained up in shackles that had spikes and razors on the inside of each cuff. Lucifer pulled out a long, serrated crimson dagger and jabbed the overweight man in the thigh and asked, "Why can't I find that blasted Rabbit? Is it really that hard to find a shape shifting trickster?"

"I–I ...wouldn't…know…" the politician stammered as sweat glistened on his greasy face.

"What good are you for then?" Lucifer growled as sliced the blade across the man's portly belly. "You *were* a person in power over millions. Surely, you must have crossed paths with Rabbit at some point in your pathetic career?"

"Please…no more…I beg…of you…mercy…" the politician croaked out as he could only watch as his entrails slowly fell out of his body.

The fallen angel grabbed him roughly by his jawline, getting mere inches from the man's face and coldly whispered, "You are in Hell, you hairless ape. The notion of mercy doesn't exist here. I'm sure that you showed a lot of mercy on Earth as people starved and suffered greatly all the while lining your greedy pockets with money that could have meant the difference between life and death for many of your constituents. How many babies did you have aborted in your lifetime, in secret, as you championed to make that procedure illegal?"

"I..." the politician cried incessantly, "I don't...know..."

"Typical." Lucifer sneered as he grabbed the portly man by his testicles. He sliced them off with one quick flick of his wrist. The political bellowed loudly but it was muted as the fallen angel shoved the man's balls into his mouth and ordered, "Shut your mouth and chew these up like a good little prick."

Tears streamed down the politician's sweaty visage as he obeyed, grimacing the entire time. A rap on Lucifer's door caught the ruler of Hell by surprise.

They know not to disturb me when I'm having fun!

"Whatever you want, it had better be important or you'll be the next one on my torture wall!" Lucifer yelled as he jabbed the politician numerous times with his crimson dagger.

The door timidly opened as an upper-level demon stepped inside. He meekly approached the fallen angel and kneeled before him and said, "My apologies for the intrusion during your soul slicing session but this couldn't wait."

"Stand up and face me!" Lucifer barked, causing the demon to flinch. "Explain to me why you shouldn't take his place."

The upper-level demon snapped to attention and replied, "Sire, *she* has been found."

Lucifer raised an eyebrow and glared, "She? Well, that narrows it down for me. Spit it out now or else."

"The trickster Rabbit has been detained, sire." The upper-level demon answered proudly.

The ruler of Hell slowly smiled as he asked, "Well done, Tuzx! Where is she being held at? I very much want to get acquainted with her."

"Not here, unfortunately. “Tuzx replied as he shifted his feet uncomfortably.

"And why isn't Rabbit here?" Lucifer retorted, his ire growing.

Tuzx rubbed the back of his neck, "The bounty hunter that caught her doesn't reside on Earth and doesn't know how to travel interdimensionally. He requested that you come and collect her. We tried to take the trickster but he killed seven of my best trackers in the process."

Lucifer thought about it, his curiosity piqued as he wondered what kind of being could dispatch seven upper-level demons. Tuzx tended to take a dozen warriors when he went on any hunt. "Very well. Take me to the bounty hunter at once."

Lucifer created a portal and said, "Put your hand on the portal and direct us to the realm. We mustn't keep this bounty hunter waiting."

Tuzx did as he was instructed and said, "Be wary of this one, sire. My warriors made the mistake of taking him lightly."

"How exactly did he best your trackers?" Lucifer asked.

"He is wicked fast and unpredictable. Probably how he caught your prize, sire." Tuzx answered as he stepped through the portal. The fallen angel sighed as he followed.

The portal opened up to a lush scenery surrounded by a forest with a great mountain range in the distance. Twenty feet away, Lucifer saw the bodies of his slain demons on the ground. Each one had their limbs severed and their abdomens sliced open, much of the ground was covered in ichor and gore.

The rest of Tuzx's trackers stood with their weapons out as they intently watched the bounty hunter. Lucifer saw a naked female lying bound at her hands and feet with a thick piece of chain connecting the bindings. The trickster had a gaping wound on her neck and she tried to kick the bounty hunter off of her back but to no avail.

The bounty hunter was dressed in a black leather jacket that came down to his calves. He was clad in form fitting leggings, a maroon shirt with a navy-blue vest and black leather boots with hair that was jet black and slicked back and appeared wet and shiny.

Lucifer noted the odd pigment of the bounty hunter's skin, which was a bright creamy pink, like that of a swine, only more pronounced. His eyes were slitted, similar to a goat, and were in the shape of tear drops and had a visage that oozed of regality. The fallen angel guessed that this being was at least three and a half feet tall but it gave off an aura of something much larger, demanding respect.

The bounty hunter looked up at Lucifer with boredom as he cleaned the bits of gore from under his gray claws with a dagger and asked, "Are you the one that placed the bounty on this wily wild game?"

"I am indeed. I'm Lucifer, what's your name, bounty hunter? I can tell that you're a demon but what else are you?"

"The name is Xander Bane. I'm what you would call a Dampire. Part demon, part vampire." The diminutive creature replied.

"May I inquire why you killed my minions?" Lucifer asked.

Xander grinned smugly as he pointed at Tuzx, "A simple miscommunication. These buffoons demanded that I hand her over without paying me for my time and effort. Naturally, I challenged them to do the dance of death with me. Your demons didn't fare so well."

Lucifer glanced at his demons and then stated, "Why not allow them to do this on my behalf. They were authorized to claim the bounty so that you could be paid. "

"This is true but I don't trust demons, let alone take their word. I figured since I couldn't get to your realm, I'd have one of your inept lackeys go fetch you." Xander said as reclined on the trickster's back. Tuzx and the other demons hissed menacingly at the Dampire but it didn't faze him.

"Get off me, you little *freak*!" Rabbit snarled, still attempting to remove Xander.

"Stop fussing. Nobody likes a sore sport. I caught your furry ass fair and square." The Dampire replied as he rolled over as whispered next to her ear, "I'm an abomination, not a freak so get your derogatory comments correct, my little delicious morsel!" Xander bit her neck again, causing her to groan painfully.

Lucifer smiled malevolently as he asked, "How is it that you managed to track her down when she eluded so many?"

The Dampire pulled his fangs out of Rabbit's neck and said, "Because I'm the best bounty hunter in all of Dragermora. It's not bragging. It's the truth, ask anyone. Although they will have a lower opinion of me. Your little darling here made the mistake of coming here wounded. I simply tasted her blood and managed to track her down easy enough, despite her shifting into a rabbit." He leaned next to her ear again and chuckled, "You taste like chicken, just so you know."

The trickster could only lull her head to the side, the loss of blood made it difficult for Rabbit to speak, let alone follow the conversation.

Xander teleported himself next to the ruler of Hell. He pulled out a scroll and held it up to Lucifer and said with a bloody grin, "I did my part, now mark this bounty with your magical signature so that I can collect my reward from the Assassin's Guild. They'll be so happy to see return there, especially Orimus."

The fallen angel touched the parchment, causing it to flare brightly as his sigil appeared on the document. Xander Bane tucked the bounty into his pocket and said as he teleported away, "Enjoy your wild game!"

Lucifer walked over and kneeled down beside Rabbit and said, "Time for you to answer for antics, trickster. Take her to Paroxysm."

"Yes, sire!" Tuzx responded as he motioned for the other demons to grab the limp woman.

They marched through the portal with Lucifer in tow. As he came through the portal, he found the she-devil waiting for him. She approached Lucifer and asked, "Is that her? The trickster?"

"It is indeed." The fallen angel replied, "I hope that you have room on your table for her. Rabbit needs your *special* attention."

"I suppose that I can somehow squeeze her in. I'll have to check my schedule to be sure," Paroxysm feigned being busy as she grinned maliciously.

"After last night, I want answers," Lucifer stated coldly, his thoughts going back to Amanda. "Break her down as often as possible. She needs to learn to *never* meddle in the affairs of Hell."

"My pleasure, sire. I'll send word when she's ready for you." Paroxysm said as she left his chamber, practically skipping.

Lucifer turned his attention to the naked politician once again as he brandished his crimson dagger once more and said with an icy grin, "It appears that I have some time to kill. Let's delve deeper into your punishment, shall we?"

******

Lucifer sat quiet in his study, reading from an ancient tome to pass the time away. The politician took the edge off but what the fallen angel wanted was to deal with the trickster. He wanted her to suffer greatly before having his own personal chat with Rabbit.

He slammed the leather-bound book closed and pushed it away, feeling bored. There was nothing to do but wait. That's the definition of Hell; eternal torture and it felt like he was on the receiving end of it. Time moves differently here. Hours on Earth are more like months in Hell.

The fallen angel paced around the study for several hours until he heard a knock on the door. He looked over as the door opened and saw Olivia standing there.

Lucifer smiled benevolently as he asked, "Hello, Olivia. What is it that you require?"

"Not me, Lucifer – er, sire?" Olivia said, feeling uneasy about how to address the ruler of Hell.

"Please, my dear. Lucifer will do just fine. Now, tell me what you desire?"

"It's Paroxysm, Lucifer. She sent me to get you. She wants you to meet her in her pain parlor." The nurse said with a hint of a smile.

The fallen angel smiled as he made his way to the door. He placed his arm around Olivia, walking with her as they made their way to Paroxysm.

He glanced down at her and asked, "Are you sure that you don't want to wait in her personal room? Paroxysm's pain parlor isn't for the faint of heart, let alone a mortal to witness."

"If I'm to be with her," Olivia answered honestly, "then I need to be exposed to everything that Paroxysm does."

Lucifer nodded. He could sense her trepidation about the torture room, but he didn't comment about it. He merely replied, "Come along then."

They walked down a long, dark staircase that led deep into the bowels of Hell itself. The screams of tortured souls reverberated loudly here. At the end of the staircase, a long corridor that consisted of solid stone with rooms on each side of the walls. Flaming orbs lit the way as they walked in tandem towards the last chamber on the right.

Lucifer opened the spiked iron gate and stepped inside. He heard Olivia gasp as she saw the condition of Paroxysm's prisoner. The trickster was sitting cross legged on a stone table, her skin peeled off and her blood coating everything around her body. Both her hands and ankles were bound with magic neutering shackles to keep her from escaping. Rabbit only looked at the fallen angel and said nothing.

"I see that you managed to break our *guest* here. Has she said anything to you?" Lucifer asked.

The she-devil looked at him, her face full of concern, "Unfortunately, that's not the case, sire. Rabbit has been silent this whole time. She transformed into a rabbit when I made the threat that I wanted to take her pelt. The only thing that she's actually said was that she will only speak to you."

"Really," Lucifer only glared at the prisoner. He moved towards her and, with a wave of his hand, made a wingback chair appear. The fallen angel sat down and asked, "What exactly is it that you want to speak to me about, Rabbit?"

"Cheesahdew."

"Pardon?" Lucifer cocked his head, puzzled by the word.

"At this point in time, my name is Cheesahdew." The prisoner spoke, her voice sounded almost crazed. "Tell me, Lucifer, did you have a holly jolly Christmas this year?"

The muscles in Lucifer's jaw twitched as his anger grew. He stood up quickly and backhanded the trickster, "What do you think, Cheesahdew? Do I look like I'm merry and having a great time?"

Cheesahdew rubbed her bloody cheek as she cackled, "I think that you hit like a fallen angel with daddy issues. Much of this night has been about that."

"What does that mean, woman?" The fallen angel growled, ready to hit her again.

"This holiday was meant to be about family and being together during the coldest night of the year. People grew closer together and took care of one another because it was about surviving winter. Now, not so much."

"What does *that* have to do with me?" Lucifer asked with a look of confusion.

Cheesahdew smiled, her teeth drenched in her own blood, "Christmas is now filled with anxiety, frustration, and stress. All because people have to find the *perfect* gift. Families are being ignored and pushed away because nobody has time for each other anymore. Hate and anger fills the air to the point that they've forgotten the meaning of the holiday, despite hearing the music and seeing the decorations that try to inspire it. Much like you, Lucifer, people use your name to sully anything terrible that happens, especially at this time of year. People push the notion that Christmas is about the birth of Jesus, even though we both know that's false. Even your own ilk never gives you the benefit of the doubt or believe that you are capable of doing good because from everyone's point of view, you are evil."

"Is there a point to all of this mad rambling, Cheesahdew?" Lucifer demanded.

"Just how *evil* is the Devil if he can leave the burning pit of Hell and grant the wishes of children across the country? I wanted to challenge not only you, but the idea that people everywhere have set in their feeble minds that even a fallen angel is capable of compassion and love, in his own way."

Lucifer's mouth gaped open. He felt shocked and stunned, as did Paroxysm and Olivia.

Cheesahdew laughed maniacally as she wiggled the spot on her forehead where her eyebrows used to be and said, "Admit it, Lucifer. You took great pride and joy playing the role of the jolly fat man this year. Do you think that all those Christmas wishes would have been answered by Santa or their families? I think not! It takes a certain kind of person to do what you did tonight so, for that, I want to thank you for playing the game."

"Is that all this was to you?" Lucifer grabbed Cheesahdew by her jaw roughly, "A bloody game? I don't appreciate being manipulated into doing anything that I don't wish to do!"

"And yet," the trickster retorted with a knowing grin, "you answered the call like it was a siren's song. You *had* the choice in this."

"This was a deal and you know that I have to respond to those!"

"You could have chosen to ignore the mailbag I sent down here." Cheesahdew said calmly. "Deep down, you know what I speak is the truth. You're not evil. You have a job to do for your Father and you do it well. It's your job to punish those that deserve it: the wicked, the cruel, and the downright evil people on Earth."

Lucifer's voice cracked ever so slightly, "I have no say in this. This is my punishment for the rebellion that I led in Heaven."

The trickster reached up and touched the ruler of Hell on the side of his angelic face, "I know. I'm the butt of many jokes to my people because my pranks never end well for me. I wanted you to have a little fun and a bit of a challenge. Something different than what you're used to doing your whole life here. Now tell me the truth, did you have a good time tonight?"

Lucifer looked away as he turned his back to the trickster. He walked over and paused, deep in thought as he recalled the events of this Christmas night. All the children that he met, the people he encountered that he managed to punish. He looked at the she-devil as she stood next to Olivia, her hand rubbing the mortal on her back lovingly.

Lucifer smiled as he spoke, "I never lie. Sure, I may bend the truth here and there, but I never lie. I did enjoy myself tonight."

Paroxysm's mouth parted in shock as she pointed, "Sire! Look at her! Look what she's doing!"

The fallen angel spun around and was surprised. The trickster glowed brightly as her flesh regenerated. Her shackles fell off as she hovered over the stone table; her cackling echoing throughout the torture chamber.

"How is this possible, sire?" The she-devil asked as she looked on in shock. "How can she release herself like that? That's not possible!"

"It's simple, she-devil," Cheesahdew answered matter of fact, "I'm a trickster as well as a minor god. Your bindings never truly cut off my magic. I'm happy that even you, Paroxysm, found happiness and love on this night. Now, I must go."

"What?" Lucifer stepped forward to stop her but he found himself frozen in place as Cheesahdew held him in place.

"I threw down the gauntlet and you answered the challenge, Lucifer. I'd say that you won so I willingly gave my pelt to your underling as a gift so that you will always remember this night. Farewell, Lucifer and be *good*." Cheesahdew said as she disappeared from the pain parlor.

Lucifer lurched forward but caught himself before he fell down. He huffed as he adjusted his jacket and vest as he spun around on his heels to leave.

"What are you going to do, sire?" Paroxysm asked meekly.

He paused at the doorway and said, "Nothing. Rabbit did what she set out to do all along. It's done and over."

"You're not mad at me?"

Lucifer glanced at the she-devil and said, "No. You did your best to contain her. How were we to know that Cheesahdew had *that* kind of power?" He nodded his head at Olivia and added, "Fret not and enjoy your lovely Christmas present."

Paroxysm let out a sigh of relief as she grabbed her nurse as murmured, "Let's get out of here and find a more suitable place to enjoy ourselves."

"Fine with me," Olivia replied, eager to leave the pain parlor.

Lucifer walked by himself back to his throne room, thinking about the conversation he had with Cheesahdew. He wasn't bothered that she escaped, especially since the trickster never was truly a prisoner.

"All just a ruse." he muttered to himself, "But to what end?"

The fallen angel clasped his hands behind his back as he slowly made his way up the staircase. His thoughts kept going back to what Rabbit had said to him.

"You had the choice in this. You could have chosen to ignore the mailbag I sent down here."

Lucifer nodded to himself as he reached the top of the staircase and turned in the direction of his throne room. Demons of various levels bowed before him as he walked by. He saw each one but didn't acknowledge any of them.

As he opened the door to his throne room, Lucifer felt like something was off. He scanned the room and saw a strange object sitting on his throne. The fallen angel marched over to it and saw that it was a decent size present. He picked it up and saw that it had a tag attached to a colorful bow that said:

To: Lucifer

From: Cheesahdew

"Great," Lucifer said out loud, "What is it this time?"

He carefully unwrapped the present, not fully trusting that the trickster wasn't playing a final prank on him. Lucifer let the paper fall harmlessly to the floor as he conjured up a table before him. He sat the strange object on the table to examine it closely.

It was a box made with clear plexiglass and had a metal tray on the inside. A stamp on the metal tray stood out to Lucifer. It was a bear paw intertwined with a wolf paw in the shape of a heart which the ruler of Hell recognized immediately.

"EnergyBear. Why not add that deity to the mix," Lucifer said to himself.

At the mention of the Cherokee deity's name, a small red button appeared on top of the box with the words *Press Me* on it in black. Lucifer was hesitant, wondering what new creation could possibly be released in Hell, like the glitter beast.

The button glowed and flashed brightly, urging the fallen angel to press it. Lucifer rolled his, recalling the last time a *gift* entered Hell from EnergyBear. It too demanded to be opened but none of his demons were brave enough to do it. The *gift* opened on its own accord and out came tons of glitter as well as the glitter beast, causing the bravest of demonic creatures to flee.

The fallen angel pressed the glowing button and waited for the antics to begin. The inside of the box filled with what Lucifer believed to be snow. Tiny balls rolled around on their own and were launched out of a small tube that materialized on the side. The snowballs flew effortlessly and out of the room.

It didn't take long for the denizens of Hell to shout loudly. One demon rushed into Lucifer's throne room and exclaimed, "Sire! We're under attack! There's strange icy beings running around throwing snowballs at us! What do we do?"

More snowballs flew from the box, heading straight for the demon. It fled the room in terror as he was bombarded with more icy projectiles. A small card popped up from the box. Lucifer snatched it up and read it.

"See, Lucifer. Snowballs do have a chance in Hell. Enjoy your gift and Merry Christmas!" – EnergyBear and Cheesahdew!

The fallen angel pinched the bridge of his nose as he shook his head.

He chuckled as the screaming of his demonic hordes filled the air and said, "Bloody Cherokee deities!"

About the Author

Joshua Griffith is a Native American Cherokee who loves to tell stories about the paranormal and the supernatural, but adds a twist of humor to alleviate some of the inherent drama and suspense that can make the characters seem more relatable. He grew up in the Eastern part of Oklahoma, witnessing many strange and wondrous things that went bump in the night. Joshua Griffith currently resides in the Pacific Northwest. As part of his path as an energy healer, Joshua Griffith felt it would be a good idea to incorporate some of his experiences in his novels. As they say, there is always a hint of truth even in a good work of fiction so it's up to you to decide which is truth and which is hot air. Joshua Griffith invites you to read his stories with an open mind because these tales are works of fiction, but ask yourself this: Could this really happen?

If you enjoyed Satan's Coming to Town, please do leave a review. If you want to see my other works, scan the QR code and it will take you to my author website. Feel free to follow and subscribe to my website, as well as my social media pages, to get future updates about new releases.

www.ingramcontent.com/pod-product-compliance
Lightning Source LLC
LaVergne TN
LVHW020539100826
845148LV00010B/1539
* 9 7 8 1 7 3 5 0 7 8 4 6 5 *